BRUSH WITH DESTINY

Other books by Mona Ingram

But Not for Me
The Reluctant Rockstar
The Shell Game

BRUSH WITH DESTINY

•

Mona Ingram

AVALON BOOKS
NEW YORK

Published by Thomas Bouregy & Co., Inc.
160 Madison Avenue, New York, NY 10016

Library of Congress Cataloging-in-Publication Data

Ingram, Mona.
  Brush with destiny / Mona Ingram.
      p. cm.
  ISBN 978-0-8034-9943-0 (hardcover : acid-free paper)
1. Women artists—Fiction.   2. Loss (Psychology)—Fiction.
3. Widowers—Fiction.   4. British Columbia—Fiction.
I. Title

 PR9199.4.I54B787 2009
 813'.6—dc22

                                           2008048217

PRINTED IN THE UNITED STATES OF AMERICA
ON ACID-FREE PAPER
BY HADDON CRAFTSMEN, BLOOMSBURG, PENNSYLVANIA

For Tracy

Thanks for believing

Chapter One

"I can do this." Ashley took several deep breaths, trying to calm the fluttering panic in her stomach. "I know I can." She glanced at the other cars in the parking lot, hopeful that no one had noticed her talking to herself. She needn't have worried. The other passengers had scurried back to their vehicles when the boarding announcement was made a couple of minutes before. The ferry attendant stood at the head of the line, walkie-talkie clipped to his fluorescent vest as he waited to motion the cars forward.

She'd been back and forth to Vancouver Island and the Gulf Islands many times, but somehow she'd never been the one driving. "There's nothing to it," her friend Jessica had assured her, brushing aside Ashley's doubts in her usual confident manner. "Just follow the car in front of you. Piece of cake."

The attendant motioned for two lines of traffic to start

up. Gesturing impatiently, he urged them forward, the cars flowing around him like a school of fish. A loud metallic clang announced the first vehicle as it drove over the heavy metal flange connecting the ferry to the wharf. Startled by the loud sound, Ashley gripped the steering wheel with both hands and moved ahead, following the directions of the next attendant. Once on the ferry, the car was plunged into shadow for a moment, then emerged into brilliant sunshine. Another attendant beckoned her forward a few extra inches, then held up his palm. Realizing she'd been holding her breath she expelled a gust of air and turned off the ignition. She'd done it!

A whimper came from the backseat and she leaned back, poking her fingers through the wire grate of the dog carrier. "You're such a good girl," she crooned as a damp nose pushed up against her fingers. "Wait a minute and I'll give you some fresh air." She unbuckled her seat belt and stepped outside, sliding back the side door of the van. "I know you hate being cooped up in there," she said, speaking softly to the wriggling dog, "but it's just a short ride." The dog quieted at the sound of her voice. It broke her heart to see the dog in the carrier, but it was safe, and the ferry ride wouldn't take all that long. "I'll be back in a little while," she said, closing the sliding door and cracking open the driver's window. "I want to watch as we pull out from the dock."

The tide was fully in and the fresh, tangy smell of the ocean drew her toward the railing. She threaded her way between the parked cars, emptying quickly of their passengers. Most people were heading for the small cafeteria, but Ashley couldn't imagine eating anything right now. Her stomach had been slightly queasy ever since she'd decided to move away from everything that had been familiar to her for so many years. It was nerves, pure and simple, but knowing that didn't make it any easier. She raised her face to the sun and a warm breeze caught a loose strand of her hair, swirling it around her face. For the first time in ages, something resembling hope surged in her heart. Her life would never be the same. She didn't kid herself about that, but was it so wrong to want to find peace? She didn't think so.

The ferry sounded its horn, the loud, jarring sound overriding the piercing calls of the seagulls. She peered over the side, fascinated by the way the sun's rays angled off into the green depths below the dock. The deck vibrated under her feet as the ferry eased away from the dock, and wash from the engines swirled seaweed growing on the pilings, revealing dozens of purple starfish clustered in the lush green growth. The bold splashes of color would appeal to Paige. . . .

She gasped for air as memories threatened to engulf her. Memories of her daughter smiling bravely up at her from the hospital bed, eyes dark and sunken, ravaged by long months of fighting the disease. Her stomach heaved and she clutched at the railing, rocking back and forth in an effort to control the sudden assault on her emotions. She'd come a long way. She knew that even without the reassuring words of the grief counselor, but sometimes, like just now, she'd forget that her precious daughter was in heaven rather than right here on earth, where she belonged. It was almost more than she could bear.

:rry picked up speed in the few minutes it took
:gain control. She raised her eyes and gazed
across the Strait of Georgia to the islands in the distance.
In the winter the seas could be rough, but today they
were surprisingly calm . . . what the fishermen called
"oily." Her artist's eye absorbed the way the islands
were darkest close up, then gradually faded to pale gray
in the distance. And yet her fingers didn't itch to pick
up a paintbrush the way they used to. That urge had disappeared when Paige had first become ill. Well-meaning
people had told her that it might help her to heal if she
could go back to painting, and she'd looked at them in
disbelief, but managed not to say what was in her heart.
That she had no idea when she'd start again. If ever.

A wisp of hair got stuck in her lipstick and she flicked
it away, recognizing as she did that her heartbeat was
returning to normal. The sea air was crisp and tangy,
and once more she told herself that she was doing the
right thing. As though to prove it, she took a few steps
closer to the bow and looked across to the group of islands, wondering which one was her future home.

"Beautiful isn't it?" A man appeared beside her, coffee cup in hand. He leaned his forearms on the railing
and gazed toward the cluster of islands. Sandy hair flut-
tered in the breeze but he didn't seem to notice. He took
a swallow of coffee, then turned to look at her, assess-
ing her steadily.

"Yes, it is. I was wondering which one is Madrona
Island."

He grinned. "You asked the right guy. I live there."

Ashley liked the way the skin around his eyes wrinkled when he smiled. He looked like someone who made his living out-of-doors, or at least spent a good deal of time outside. She hadn't given much thought to the types of people she would meet on the island, and although it was too soon to make any judgments, she took his open, friendly nature as a good sign.

"Which one is it?" She squinted against the sun. The islands folded in on one another.

"Kind of hard to tell from here, but the ferry will take us to starboard around that first big island and then we'll head east, to the terminal. I'll show you when we get closer, if you like."

"I'd like that." She hesitated. "Have you lived there long?"

A fleeting shadow passed across his eyes and she wondered if she'd imagined it. "About nine years." He scrubbed a hand across his face. "Doesn't seem possible, somehow."

"You must like it then."

"Yeah, we do." He hiked his thumb back over his shoulder. "I'm bringing a bicycle home for my daughter. It's in the truck."

Ashley flinched inside at the mention of his daughter. "She'll be excited about that."

He rolled his eyes. "Tell me about it. Her little girlfriend got one last month and I haven't had a moment's peace since." He drained the coffee from his cup. "Listen, can I get you a coffee or something? You know, to welcome you to the island?"

Ashley stepped back. "No thanks. Really." She looked back at the van. "I should see to my dog. She doesn't like being left alone."

"So that's what you were doing. I'm parked in the next row over, a bit behind you, and I saw you when you got out and started talking to something in the car." His eyes crinkled again and he pushed away from the railing. "Caitlin has been angling for a dog for a couple of years now, but we're hoping the bike will keep her occupied for a while."

Ashley turned and they walked along the railing back toward their vehicles. "Well, if she's still asking for a dog next year or the year after you'll know she's really interested. Too many parents buy dogs for their kids before they're really prepared to care for them." She waved a hand. "Sorry. I shouldn't be so opinionated."

"No, I'm glad to hear you say that, and I agree." They came to the van. "May I see your dog? Truth is, I'd love to have one myself."

Ashley quickly opened the side door and leaned over, putting her face near the cage. "Here's my sweet girl." She turned her head and smiled up at the stranger. "I'd introduce you, but I don't know your name."

He extended his hand. "Matt."

Ashley shook his hand, expecting to find it callused and was surprised that it wasn't. "Ashley," she said, keeping the introduction light and informal. "And this is Honey." The honey-colored cocker spaniel cocked her head at the mention of her name. "Not a very original name I'm afraid. I rescued her from the SPCA quite a few years ago and I've never regretted it for a minute."

"She's a sweetheart." Matt held the back of his fingers up to the cage so the dog could pick up his scent. "Are you moving into a house or one of those new condos?"

Ashley waved a hand in front of her face. "Not those condos. No. Never." She was rewarded with a broad grin. "I take it you don't care for them either."

"I think they're a blight on our island."

"I agree. Ever since I decided to move there I've been keeping up with the debate in the local newspaper and I'm glad that they've declared a moratorium on that type of development."

"Where did you buy?"

"Oh, I didn't buy. I found a wonderful deal through Brenda Kerr."

He nodded his approval. "I know Brenda. She's an excellent Realtor."

"I've found a waterfront place that I've leased for six months, and I have an option for an additional six months plus first refusal if they put it on the market."

"Wow. That *is* a good deal. Where is it?"

"Near Luna Bay. Southwest exposure. It looks great from the pictures I've seen."

"You mean you haven't actually seen it?"

Ashley ducked her head. "Sounds crazy, doesn't it? But no, I haven't seen it in person, although she sent lots of pictures."

"Well, good luck with it." He pointed over her shoulder. "Look, we've rounded the point and you can see Madrona now. The ferry terminal is tucked in that bay ahead of us."

Ashley scanned the shoreline, impressed at the size

of some of the homes. "Wow, look at those places. The owners must have pretty deep pockets."

"A lot of them are second homes owned by people who live and work in Vancouver during the week and come over for the weekend."

The ferry drew closer to the terminal and Ashley could see two lines of cars parked on the steep incline waiting to board the ferry. Creosote-covered pilings anchored the dock, and the ferry started to shudder as it slowed.

"I'd better get back to my vehicle. I apologize for monopolizing your time." He grinned again. "I hope you enjoy living on the island."

"Thanks." She watched him dodge between the vehicles, the top of his golden head easily visible over the roofs of the cars. It was hard not to envy him, going home to his family. She gave her head a quick shake, climbed into her van, and snapped on her seat belt. Digging her cell phone out of her bag she called the Realtor, who agreed to meet her at her new home with the key. "Turn your odometer to zero and follow the signs to Luna Bay. It's a little over three and a half miles from the terminal. I checked the other day." The ferry pulled between the pilings, bumping gently from side to side, signaling their arrival. She turned to check on Honey. "I should have prepared a little speech or something. After all, it's not every day two girls like us start a new chapter in their lives." The dog gave an answering bark, as though understanding Ashley's words.

Ashley laughed. "You said it." The ramp lowered and she turned the key in the ignition. "Okay, here we go."

In a matter of moments she'd driven off the ferry and

climbed the steep roadway, caught up in the flow of traffic. She smiled to herself when she realized that this was the closest thing she would find to a traffic jam on this small island. Not wanting to cloud her first impressions of her new home, she pulled off to the side of the road to let the other cars pass. Within minutes there were no vehicles visible in her rearview mirror and with a sigh of relief she lowered her window and pulled out onto the road. Afternoon sunlight angled in shafts through tall firs, flickering against her face as she drove along. The road was paved but narrow, affording tantalizing glimpses of ocean between stands of trees. Then it swung back inland and Ashley was surprised to see open fields to her left. An ancient apple orchard covered a south-facing slope and she longed to stop and enjoy the sight of the gnarled trees, still lovingly tended, but that would have to wait for another day. Beyond the orchard an old farmhouse was partly visible at the end of a long driveway. It was covered in scaffolding and painters were busy applying chalk-white paint and red trim. In happier days the orchard and farmhouse would have inspired a painting. She gave herself a mental slap. It was better not to dwell on the past. Coming to a junction in the road she took the right-hand turn and followed the sign toward Luna Bay.

The house number was clearly indicated on a post alongside the road and Ashley turned, driving between massive cedars as she made her way down toward the house. Her vehicle made almost no noise on the soft earth and she breathed deeply, unsure which smelled better—the breeze off the ocean or the dark, musty smell of years of vegetation. All she knew was that both smells brought a sense of peace and once more she knew she'd made the right decision.

"Welcome!" She recognized Brenda from her picture on the Web site as the Realtor came out of the house, her hand extended. "I'm delighted to meet you."

"Thank you." Ashley liked Brenda instantly. "If you'll excuse me, I'll just let my dog out. She's been cooped up in there for a few hours now."

"Isn't she lovely." Brenda watched as Ashley clipped a lead to Honey's collar and set her on the driveway. The dog immediately commenced sniffing around, looking for signs of other dogs. "Looks as though she likes it already."

"I hope so." Ashley lifted her head and looked at the house and grounds for the first time. The driveway circled a green space rimmed with flower beds. In the center of the grass, a dogwood tree was in full bloom, the flowers tinged with pale pink. The house was set into the hillside, flanked on one side by a rocky outcropping. Dotted across the surface of the rock, indigenous plants thrived in crevices where organic material had collected over the years. On the right side of the house, a magnificent arbutus tree spread its branches like a benediction, its thick glossy leaves gleaming in the sun. Its trunk, where the bark had peeled away, was a rich cinnamon color in the afternoon sun.

"It's . . . I don't know what to say." Ashley was on the verge of tears. "I love it already and I haven't even seen inside the house." She turned to Brenda. "I can't imagine anyone owning this and not wanting to live here."

The Realtor nodded her agreement. "The owners are a wonderful old couple, but they've moved to Victoria to be closer to their grandchildren." She led Ashley around the side of the house and indicated a steep stairway to a small beach below. "They just can't get around anymore, especially down there." She led Ashley up onto a deck. "Come on—I'll show you the inside."

The home was everything Ashley had expected, and more. A fieldstone fireplace took up one wall of the living room, and windows overlooked the ocean. Just off the living room a glass-enclosed sunroom would make an ideal studio. Sunlight spilled onto the floor in a corner of the room, a perfect spot for Honey's basket. The dog loved to curl up in the sunshine for her afternoon snooze.

The kitchen had been completely remodeled with top-of-the-line appliances and granite countertops. A small bathroom and guestroom occupied the balance of the space on the main level and the upstairs loft contained a huge bedroom and ensuite bathroom.

"I'll be able to see the ocean first thing when I wake up." Ashley could hardly believe her good luck. "Everything is just as you said. It's not very big, but then who needs more rooms when you have that for a view?" She stood at the loft railing and, as though on cue, a sailboat shot past the rocky outcrop to the right of the house, on a tack toward open ocean. It heeled over as a gust of wind snapped the sails taut, a frothy wake trailing behind.

"It doesn't get any better than this. Thank you again for finding it for me."

The Realtor led her back downstairs and they completed the necessary paperwork. "I've left you some tea, coffee, bread, eggs, things like that to get you started." Ashley had noticed a bowl of fruit on the counter. "I thought you may not feel like going out tonight."

Ashley picked up the dog, her fingers absently combing the animal's coat. "That's very thoughtful. I am a bit tired."

"Oh, and I left you a map of the island, with some of the stores marked. Grocery store, hardware, pharmacy." She tapped the map. "They're mostly located in our little mall and there's a farmers' market there every Saturday morning."

"Sounds like fun." She walked with the Realtor to the door. "Thanks again, Brenda. I'll be in touch."

Ashley walked slowly back into the house and was drawn to the sliding doors leading to the broad deck. Wide steps led down to a small landing where the stairs to the beach started. Honey padded over to the edge of the landing and looked over, then back up at Ashley. "Not today," she said, studying the small beach at the bottom of the stairs. At the far end, sheltered by a small headland, layers of what appeared to be sandstone held small tidal pools, their still water reflecting the blue of the sky. The rest of the beach was made up of coarse sand, while strands of kelp and small logs marked the extent of high tide. How Paige would have loved this beach!

Suddenly legless, Ashley stumbled back and sat down on one of the wide steps. Tears pooled in her eyes and she didn't try to stop them, didn't wipe them away. They streamed down her face unchecked and Honey whimpered beside her, burrowing under her arm and pressing her warm body against Ashley's side. Ashley looked down at the dog. "You miss her too, don't you, girl?" She held the dog to her side and stared unseeing at the sparkling water below, her thoughts drifting back to the day over eleven years ago when Paige had been born. Lashed by an early winter storm, she'd made her way to the hospital alone, confident that she had plenty of time. She hadn't been able to reach Doug but that wasn't unusual and she found that she didn't really mind. He constantly made comments about her independence, and that was one day she was grateful that she'd been raised to think for herself. He'd arrived an hour after his daughter was born, full of apologies.

The dog squirmed and Ashley let her go, realizing that she had tightened her grip around the small animal. Releasing her hair from the silk scarf that held it in place, she shook it out and continued her reverie. She hadn't thought about it before, but the day Paige was born was probably the beginning of the end of her marriage. She just hadn't realized it at the time. When their daughter was a baby they'd tried to make the marriage work, and later, when Paige became ill, their love for her had kept them together. After Paige died the divorce had seemed like an inevitable link in the heartbreaking chain of events. The marriage had been over a long time, but the pain of their daughter's death had left them both emotionally spent. The final separation had been remarkably civil.

An unfamiliar sound broke the silence and the dog's head snapped around. A high, piercing call preceded the arrival of a bald eagle, riding an air current so close to the house that Ashley could look into its eyes as it turned its head to look at her. It approached a dead tree toward the end of the beach, extending its talons to grip a bare branch and folding broad wings as it came to rest.

Ashley stood up. "That's our sign to start unpacking." The dog seemed to understand, and led her on the walkway around the side of the house to the van.

Within forty-five minutes the van had been emptied of its contents. Boxes and suitcases were stacked haphazardly around the room, but Ashley was content. She had even set up her easel and unpacked a few of her paints and brushes. The rest of her equipment was tucked into the storage space under the stairs. Honey's basket sat on the floor nearby and her food and water dishes looked at home on a mat in the kitchen.

Ashley stood back to admire her new surroundings, but her gaze was drawn outside to the arbutus tree. No longer in the direct sunlight, it was still a compelling sight, smooth trunk contrasting dramatically with bark hanging in curling strips. Her hand drifted unconsciously over a container of brushes, fingering the soft sable.

She missed painting. She picked up a bottle of linseed oil. The pungent smell reminded her how much she enjoyed everything about the creative process. Her gaze went back to the tree and the sparkling ocean beyond. There was something peaceful about being here, and the tense muscles in her neck and shoulders started to relax. For the first time in several years, her fingers tingled, a sure sign that a new painting wouldn't be too far away.

In the early years of her career, Doug hadn't taken much notice when she'd sold the odd canvas through a small gallery in North Vancouver. He'd never discouraged her, but neither had he done anything to boost her confidence. As partner in a high-powered law firm, he'd considered her painting little more than a hobby.

And perhaps it had been, at first. But then the gallery had been bought by a dynamic businesswoman from Montreal, and Ashley's life had taken a dramatic turn.

She could still remember Gabrielle's reaction the first time she'd delivered a new batch of paintings. She'd been hesitant, unsure of how the new owner would view her work.

"These are *formidable*!" the Frenchwoman had stated enthusiastically. "You have talent, *chérie*."

"Well, I don't know." Ashley looked around the gallery, noticing that it was being expanded.

Gabrielle had lit an unfiltered cigarette and looked at her through a haze of smoke. She absently picked a fleck of tobacco from her lip and examined the paintings more carefully, seemingly lost in thought. Her eyes narrowed. "Has no one ever told you how good you are?"

Ashley didn't know how to take this forceful woman, so she told her the truth. "No, not really."

"Tsk, tsk." Cigarette ashes dropped onto the hardwood floor but Gabrielle didn't seem to notice. "*Quel dommage*," she said, then translated, "What a pity." She walked back to the paintings and studied them again, but Ashley had a feeling that Gabrielle wasn't really looking. She was thinking.

After a few moments she turned. "Do you have any more finished paintings at home?" She gestured to the small pile in front of her. "Similar to these?"

"Oh, yes." Ashley's confidence swelled. "I have about ten more and a couple I'm working on."

Gabrielle nodded to herself. "*Bien.*" She looked Ashley in the eye. "If you will allow me to represent you, I would like to put together a proposal for you. These paintings are ideal for a calendar and for notecards." She stubbed out the cigarette and leaned on the worktable, dark eyes watching Ashley intently. "We can try each other out on this project. I'll be your representative and I will fight for your rights but I will never put any pressure on you. If we like working together we can put it in writing sometime in the future."

Ashley had looked down at the paintings on the worktable, then back up at Gabrielle. "If you really think they're good enough." She was having a difficult time taking it all in. Maybe she was dreaming.

"Believe me. They're good enough." Gabrielle extended her hand. "I'll put something together and get back to you." She paused. "I think one day you're going to be very famous."

Chapter Two

Gabrielle had been right. Today Ashley's work was very much in demand, and she'd stopped marveling at the size of the checks from contracts that the gallery owner had agented over the years. The Frenchwoman had an eye for new talent, and had promoted several other promising artists as well. The best part about working with her was that she was true to her word. She never pushed. She would laugh in that husky smoker's voice, saying that she understood the artistic temperament.

Doug refused to understand her loyalty to the woman who had "discovered" her. "You don't owe her anything," he'd rail. "You owe it to yourself to go with somebody bigger. Someone who can swing a better deal."

But her loyalty to Gabrielle had never wavered and she'd resisted his constant pressure. Finally he'd stopped trying to control her career. That was another thing she could be thankful for now that she was alone.

Her phone rang, breaking into her thoughts and yanking her back to the present. She fumbled in her purse, delighted to see that the caller was Jessica.

It suddenly hit her that her friend wasn't a ten-minute drive away anymore. "Hi, Jess." Her voice trembled but she didn't try to control it. She'd grown up with Jessica Burns and they had no secrets from each other. "How did the interview go?"

"It went well, but I was a bit distracted thinking I should have been with you." A journalist with one of Canada's major newspapers, Jessica covered the political beat. Today's interview had been with the Australian prime minister, and she'd been lucky to get it. "But I know what you're going to say. You had to do this part for yourself. So tell me, how is the house?"

"It's wonderful." Ashley sank into an overstuffed chair, noticing the top-quality furniture for the first time. "But you'll be seeing it for yourself tomorrow." She hesitated. "That is, if you're still coming?"

"You just try and keep me away. I'll write my story in the morning and I'll be on the two o'clock ferry. You're still going to pick me up, right? No sense getting in that lineup when I can walk right on as a foot passenger."

"I agree, and I'll be there. See you around three."

"Sleep well tonight."

Ashley chuckled. "You too. See you tomorrow." She disconnected and headed to the kitchen to see what she could find to eat.

White light filled the loft the next morning and Ashley looked outside to see the beginnings of a perfect day. Sunlight bounced off the water, almost blinding her with its brilliance. After a quick shower she dug through her suitcase and found a long cotton skirt she hadn't worn in years. She combined it with a simple scoop-neck top and tied back her hair with a matching ribbon. One last check of her shopping list and she was out the door and in her ear, Honey jumping in alongside her.

The little mall was easy to find. As Brenda had explained, there was one major road around the island and points of interest were well marked. Ashley's attention was drawn to gaily colored tents at one end of the parking lot. Tourists in their crisp new clothes mingled with locals, inspecting the offerings. "The Country Market," she said aloud to Honey. "Shall we go have a look?" She found a parking space and, after getting out of the car, the little dog trotted obediently beside her, happy to be outside in new surroundings.

A variety of goods were on sale. Several jewelry vendors offered exquisitely crafted original pieces, another displayed homemade soaps and candles, and others sold knit goods, freshly baked cookies, and cakes. She paused at one stand to admire some children's toys made of wood.

"You've taken a lot of care with these," she said, running her fingers over the smooth edges of the toys. The older gentleman on the other side of the table smiled in acknowledgment and continued to puff away at his pipe. The smoke was sweet, and reminded Ashley of her grandfather. At the next stand, she bought some locally produced honey, as well as candles made from honey-comb. Under a massive fir tree, a man sang and played guitar, his CDs for sale in a basket at his feet. This was unlike the rigid, strictly controlled markets she'd sometimes visited in the city. Here, friends met and chatted, frequently drifting off to sit at one of the nearby picnic tables and have coffee. Children and dogs played on the grass while parents shopped. A smile touched her lips as she thought of how Paige would have fit right in.

An impressive array of vegetables decorated the next table. Plump red radishes begged to be purchased and she reached for a bunch, as well as a bunch of green onions.

"Well, hello there." A man's voice greeted her, deep and familiar.

She looked up, startled. It was the man from the ferry. He stood behind the counter, hands in his pockets, looking uncomfortable.

"Oh, hello. Nice to see you again." And it was, she thought to herself, surprised by her reaction. He looked like he'd just stepped out of the shower and run his fingers though his hair. "Matt, isn't it?"

A broad grin transformed his face and she couldn't help noticing his perfect teeth. And those laugh lines around his eyes. Here under the canopy of the tent his eyes looked dark, but she thought she remembered them as being an intense blue. She gave herself a quick mental shake. What was she doing looking at him like a love-starved teenager? She flushed and lowered her head, pretending to inspect a perfectly spaced row of lettuce. "So, this is your stand," she said, keeping her voice light. "You have a real knack for displaying your wares."

He chuckled and took her purchases, placing them in a used plastic bag. "I hope you don't mind, but my daughter insists on recycling." He accepted her money and counted out the change. "I'm sure Caitlin will appreciate your compliment. It's her stand." He scanned the adjacent parking lot. "She's around here somewhere. Schmoozing, no doubt."

"She's here?" Ashley scanned the crowd.

"Yeah, here she comes." A small child with dark hair appeared at Ashley's side and immediately went down on her knees beside Honey.

"Hello," she said somberly, as though addressing another child. Small fingers petted the top of the dog's head, then caressed the large ear. "What's your name, little dog?" She looked up with dark green eyes, and Ashley's breath caught in her throat. This child was only slightly older than Paige had been when she was first diagnosed.

"Her name is Honey." Matt stepped around from behind the table. "Caitlin, this is the lady I was telling you about yesterday. The one I met on the ferry."

The child studied her for a moment, then smiled. "Daddy brought me a bike."

Ashley found her voice. "I know— he told me about it. Do you like it?"

"I love it," Caitlin said with an emphatic nod. "Now Kimberly and I can ride around the island anytime we like." She glanced up at her father. "As long as we tell someone where we're going."

Matt was still holding the bag with Ashley's purchases

and Caitlin seemed to notice the table for the first time. "Daddy, please. I told you, you have to make things look nice." She bustled back to her place behind the counter and started to rearrange the produce in neat little rows. "People like it when things look nice."

Matt rolled his eyes. "Ten going on thirty," he said to Ashley in a stage whisper.

"I'm almost eleven." The child paused, a bunch of radishes in one hand. "Will you be coming again next week? Maybe I could play with your dog."

Ashley was startled by the rapid change in direction of the conversation. "Yes, I'll probably be back next week." She looked around. "This is a relaxing way to shop. As a matter of fact there are still a few stalls I haven't checked out yet."

Caitlin squatted down again and buried her face in Honey's coat. " 'Bye, Honey. See you next week."

"Thanks for stopping by." Matt handed her the bag of produce. "Enjoy the rest of your day."

A local nursery had a stall set up and Ashley bought a hanging basket as a gift for Brenda and ordered two large flowering planters for the outside deck.

"Is there any way you could deliver these?" Ashley asked.

"Not today." The young man behind the table counted out her change. "Saturday's a busy day, but I'd be glad to bring them out to you tomorrow. My name's Don, by the way." He jotted down her address. "See you tomorrow."

Pleased with her purchases, Ashley wandered into

the grocery store and quickly filled her basket with items from her shopping list.

She was making her way to her car when she heard footsteps hurrying to catch up with her.

"Ashley." Matt drew even and she stopped. "I was wondering if you'd like to have that cup of coffee?" His smile was open. "You know, the one I offered yesterday on the ferry to welcome you to the island." He indicated picnic tables under a group of trees and gestured toward a coffee shop. "I can offer you a decent latté, if that's your pleasure."

"That sounds tempting but I'm sorry I can't. I just bought some ice cream and I'd better get it home before it melts."

"In that case, I'll help you load your groceries." He pushed the cart toward her van and quickly moved the bags into the back, following her directions. "Tell you what," he said cheerfully as she climbed into the driver's seat. "Caity and I usually go to the marina for lunch on market days. They make a fabulous hamburger. If you'd like to join us, you're welcome. We'll get there by one o'clock." He backed away from the window. "Just follow the main road past Luna Bay and you'll see the signs leading to the marina."

He stuck his hands in the back pockets of his jeans and she couldn't help but notice the way they molded to his body. She tore her eyes away and put the van in reverse. "I'm still unpacking and I have company coming this afternoon so I don't think I could make it, but thanks for the invitation."

He gave a casual shrug. "If you finish early . . ." He let the words trail off.

Matt watched the van pull out of the parking lot. He didn't know why he'd pursued her like that. Or did he? Yesterday on the ferry he'd watched her for a few minutes before going to stand beside her. She'd looked like she was crying, or was about to, so he'd waited until she pulled herself together before approaching. There was something about this woman that appealed to him but he couldn't say what that was. She was small and delicate, and from the first moment he'd had the strongest desire to get to know her . . . to shelter her from whatever was troubling her.

"Cut it out, Matt," he murmured to himself and headed toward the coffee shop.

Coffee in hand, he headed toward his vehicle. It had become his habit to use the hours of the market to do some work and today he had reports to read. He waved at Caitlin as he passed her stand, indicating where he was going. The hours spent here were long, but not wasted. As a matter of fact, in his opinion the market served two purposes. Gardening had been a great passion of Caitlin's from the time she could dig in the soil, and when she'd expressed an interest in growing produce and selling it, he'd supported her. It pleased him that his daughter wasn't going to be one of those children who thought that lettuce came from the grocery store. The other benefit was that she'd shown a true entrepreneurial spirit, keeping track of her sales and expenditures. Her little spiral-bound booklet already had many pages bearing neat columns of figures.

Chuckling to himself, he settled down to work. Fortunately, he'd always been able to concentrate and he was thankful for that ability. Today it would have been too easy to let his mind drift . . . to think about Ashley, to wonder what had caused the sadness that was so evident behind those brown eyes. He took a deep breath and turned his attention to a company report.

"Ashley, you shouldn't have." Brenda graciously accepted the hanging basket. "But since you did, I have just the place for it." She took it outside and hung it on a bracket. "Business has been so brisk this spring I haven't had time to get one." The bracket was strategically placed so the plant did not cover the real estate sign. "Now that looks a lot better."

"I'm glad you like it. I just wanted to say that I appreciate your thoughtfulness." Ashley looked across the road to the marina and the sparkling waters of Luna Bay beyond. "You know, as recently as yesterday, coming over here on the ferry, I still wasn't sure if this move was right for me. But this morning I'm beginning to believe that I'll fit right in." She gestured toward the marina. "What's not to like?"

"Well, it's easy to fall in love with this place in the sunshine, but the winters can get raw." Brenda's gaze drifted over the sailboats and powerboats in the marina. "Surprisingly enough, winter is when this island really comes into its own. That's when we become a community again 'cause that's when we look out for one another. In the summer, when the population quadruples with tourists, those of us who work hardly see our friends. But in the winter we pull together as a group, and some of the best entertainment is what we create ourselves." She tilted her head, looked at Ashley speculatively. "After you're settled, you might like to join the Madrona Players—our little theater group. Now *there's* a real cross-section of island people. You might enjoy it."

"Oh no. I could never do anything like that. I'd be tongue-tied."

"Actually, I was thinking of you for some of the more creative aspects. Set building, set design, painting. You'd be great at that."

Ashley shot her a cautious look. She hadn't told anyone that she was an artist, and she wondered at Brenda's oblique reference to painting.

The Realtor continued talking. "You'd be amazed at some of the effects a clever set painter can create."

"I probably would." Ashley hesitated. "But I don't know . . ."

Brenda held up a hand. Her smile was kind. "I'm not about to 'out' you as a famous painter. As far as I know I'm the only one who knows who you are. I haven't told anyone else." She shrugged. "It's a small island with a small population but we have several fairly famous people here. Namely writers, but in my opinion they're here for a reason. Nobody bothers them. If they wanted publicity they'd be living large on the mainland."

Ashley nodded. "I suppose so. I'm not really all that

famous, you know, but I'd appreciate it if you didn't mention me to anyone. I'd like to get the feel of the place first and if I decide to join your little theater group I could just introduce myself as Ashley."

"Not a problem. Tell you what, I'll put your name on the list of people who might be interested and when we have our first meeting of the season someone will give you a call. Now, do you have time for a cup of coffee?"

"Thanks but I have a friend coming over from Vancouver this afternoon and I still haven't finished unpacking. There is one thing you could help me with, though. Is there someone you could recommend to look in on my dog if I go away for a day or two? I like to leave her in the house."

"I know the perfect person. Gloria Anderson. Come on in and I'll give you her phone number."

Ashley tucked the number into her bag. "Thanks again, Brenda, and now I'd better get home." She brightened. "Did you hear that? I called it home already."

Brenda laughed. "We'll make an islander of you yet."

Ashley drove away with a smile on her lips. She'd smiled more this morning than she had in a long time, and it felt good.

"Well, what do you think?" Ashley flattened the last of the boxes and turned to Honey. There hadn't been much to unpack. She'd brought only a few personal items; treasured photos of her daughter and a few pieces from her colored glass collection now brightened the windowsills in the sunroom. She had a box full of craft projects that Paige had completed over the years but it was too soon to display them. Perhaps later, when the memories had softened a bit more. In the meantime, the familiar items lent an air of stability and she looked around, wondering how the house would appear to Jessica. She glanced at her watch. A quarter to one and Jessica's ferry wouldn't be pulling in until three. A long time to wait.

She wandered out onto the deck and stretched out on one of the lounges while Honey flopped down at the head of the stairs. The arbutus tree raised its branches to the sky and sunlight filtered down through the leaves, spangling the deck with gold coins of light. Ashley was admiring the rich color of the trunk when she heard an unfamiliar sound just over her head. *Zzzt.* She looked up, unable to see what had made the noise. Once again the sound startled her. A tiny hummingbird hovered in front of her, inspecting the bright swirls of color in her skirt. It moved sideways, and a shaft of sunlight transformed the feathers under the throat from dark to fluorescent orange-red. Stifling a gasp, she watched in amazement as the bird darted to a shrub and dipped its beak into the flowers, a tiny drop of nectar glistening at the tip. It left as quickly as it had appeared, leaving her wide-eyed with delight. Honey hadn't even noticed the bird. She was asleep, snuffling softly, her golden head on outstretched paws.

"That's it." Ashley jumped up and gathered Honey in her arms. She took the animal inside and placed her in her basket where she looked up questioningly then snuggled down and went back to sleep. Ashley grabbed her bag and a straw hat and hurried to the door. The clock in the van indicated three minutes to one; she'd only be a few minutes late. It would do her good to meet Matt and his daughter for lunch, and besides, she owed herself a treat after unpacking so swiftly.

She slowed the vehicle and pulled over to the side of the road. What was she doing? All she knew about Matt was that he lived here on the island and that he had a daughter. Where was his wife in all this? She thought back to the two conversations she'd had with him and couldn't recall him mentioning a wife. Odd perhaps, but it probably didn't mean anything . . . or did it? One thing was sure—sitting here on the side of the road wasn't going to bring her the answer. She pulled out again and headed toward the marina.

Minutes later she pulled into the parking lot. It was almost full of cars and trucks—a surprising number for such a small island. She was glad she'd worn flat sandals as she made her way across the gravel toward the ramp. It tilted down precipitously and she realized that the tide must be out. Pausing at the head of the ramp she surveyed the marina, tucked into a sheltering cove. The number of boats moored at the docks was staggering. There was no way she could estimate the millions of dollars tied up here. As she watched, several boats headed out into the strait. They were under power now, but soon their sails would fill with air and they'd join the myriad other sailboats in some of the most pristine waters in the world.

"Excuse me." A young couple waited behind her and she realized she was blocking the ramp leading down to the dock. "Sorry," she said, standing aside, then followed them down, gripping the railing with one hand and her hat with the other. She kept her eyes on the ramp, stepping cautiously until she reached the bottom.

Lifting her eyes, she looked around for Matt. Several groups of people looked her way but nobody looked familiar. She scanned the crowd once again, more surprised than disappointed that Matt hadn't shown up. *They must have changed their minds*, she thought, but she was here now, so she might as well get something to eat.

"Can I help you with something?" Ashley turned to see a waitress heading toward one of the picnic tables, bearing a tray heaped with platters of hamburgers and drinks.

"Uh, I don't know. I was supposed to meet some friends, but they don't seem to be here." Ashley looked around again, as though expecting Matt to appear out of thin air.

"Well, you're welcome to wait for them if you'd like. There's a table free over there." The waitress nodded. "I'll just deliver this and be right back."

Ashley hesitated, then sat down, feeling somewhat foolish. She could always have a hamburger by herself. There were times, like right now, when she couldn't quite accept that she was on her own, that she'd have to do things by herself from now on. But that was what she'd wanted, wasn't it? A chance to be by herself, to learn to live again? With a sigh she sat back and ordered a drink from the waitress as she came by. She might as well enjoy the setting. A sleek sailboat was pulling out and she watched as a young woman came up from below and stood beside a suntanned man, who slipped his arm around her waist as they exited the harbor. Ashley wondered idly if she would ever sail again. She could easily afford to buy a small sailboat, but sailing alone wasn't something that interested her. And she'd never felt more alone than she did right now.

"I had a good day today, Daddy." Caitlin skipped across the parking lot, trying to keep up with her father. "I made forty-four dollars and fifty cents."

Matt smiled to himself. Caitlin had picked up the lingo of the vendors, who talked among themselves at the end of each market day. A "good day" meant happy vendors who would go home and start preparing for the next market. "That's good, princess. I'm glad it went well, but did you have to take so long packing up?"

"But, Daddy, I had to be polite to the man from the inn. He wants to try out my butter lettuce for a couple of weeks."

Matt's thoughts flew ahead. "We're going to need a bigger compost pile."

"Why do you say that?" Caitlin stopped, looking up at him curiously.

"Because you grow the best butter lettuce on the planet. That means he'll want lots more next year. That means a bigger garden." He sighed dramatically. "Where will it end?"

"You're silly." Caitlin giggled and started down the ramp.

Matt checked his watch. One-thirty. He shaded his eyes and checked the picnic tables. At that moment

Ashley removed her hat and he recognized her instantly. "She came," he told himself, drinking in the sight of her. Her hair rippled down her back and he found himself wondering how it would feel between his fingers. He hurried down the ramp, easily catching up with Caitlin.

Chapter Three

"**D**addy, there's nowhere to sit." Ashley heard a child's voice and turned, ready to give up her table. Matt was striding toward her, and he grabbed Caitlin's hand as they approached.

"You came," he said with a lopsided grin that tugged at Ashley's heart. "I'm sorry we're late, but Caitlin had some important business to take care of."

Caitlin gave her an odd look, then seemed to accept her presence. "I'm going to sell some lettuce to the inn. Did you bring Honey?"

Ashley glanced at Matt, wondering how long it had taken him to adjust to the way the child's mind darted from one topic to another. "No. She was having a nap when I left home." She hesitated. "Older dogs need more sleep. Sort of like people, I guess."

Caitlin frowned. "Is she going to die?"

Ashley pulled back, startled. "Heavens no. Well, not

for quite a few years, I hope. I think she's about eight right now. That's middle-aged for a dog."

Caitlin thought for a moment then her face brightened. "Okay." She turned to Matt. "Can I go look for Kimberly? I saw her father's car in the lot."

"Yes, but be careful, and no running on the dock. You know the rules. Do you want your usual?"

"Yes, please." The child smiled brightly then was gone.

Matt's eyes softened as he watched her go. "She's a little whirlwind, but I wouldn't have it any other way. Ah, she's found her friend. Now I can rest easy." He turned his attention back to Ashley.

"Ashley, what is it?" He leaned forward and she pulled back, brushing away the tears that threatened to spill down her cheeks.

"I'm sorry," she said, attempting to smile, knowing it came across as more of a grimace. "It's just . . ." she waved a hand in front of her face. "I'm sorry."

"Is it something I said?" A gust of wind lifted a chunk of his hair and Ashley tried to focus on it. She didn't think she could bear to look in his eyes, to see the concern that was so evident in his voice.

"No." Her gaze drifted past Matt to the far side of the marina where Caitlin was engaged in an animated conversation with her friend. "It's your daughter." She dragged her eyes away from the girls and forced herself to look at the man across the table.

"But she didn't say anything . . ." His voice trailed off. He was confused and she didn't blame him.

"No." She seemed to be saying that a lot. She had to explain but she didn't know if she could get the

words to come out. It struck her then that she hadn't actually told anyone about Paige. Those who knew had
been told by someone else in an effort to make things
easier for her. She took a deep breath. "It's just that
your daughter—" She took a deep shuddering breath.
"Your daughter reminds me so much of my own." She
took the straw from her drink and crumpled it in her
hand. Matt didn't move.

"My daughter was nine when she was diagnosed
with leukemia." She looked at the straw as though wondering where it had come from, then dropped it onto
the table. "I knew that leukemia was a serious disease,
but never for a moment did I consider that Paige would
die. She had the best of care, the best doctors, and yet at
the end she was beaten by the disease." She picked up
her glass but her hands were shaking. She set it down
again, but continued to hold it, her knuckles white with
tension. When she spoke again her voice was raw, little
more than a whisper. "We were all beaten by it."

She looked up then to find him watching her. "I'm
sorry," he said simply. "Do you mind if I ask you how
long ago?"

"It's been almost three years." She pried her fingers
away from the glass. "Thirty-four months, and in some
ways it feels like it was yesterday. You can't imagine
what it feels like to watch your child battle so valiantly.
You see these children on television programs or in
movies. They're always so brave and they're the ones
who support their parents instead of the other way
around. That part is real, believe me." She fished in her
purse for a Kleenex, then dabbed at her eyes and gave

him a tentative grin. "I'm sorry for dumping on you, but that's the first time I've told anyone about Paige."

"Hello, Matt. Shame on you for keeping your friend waiting." The waitress set a cup of coffee down in front of Matt and winked at Ashley. If she noticed the red eyes she didn't say anything. "How did the market go today? I saw Caitlin go flying by a bit earlier."

"Hi, Chris. The market was good and Caity's pumped about a new customer. Frank from the inn wants to try some of her butter lettuce."

"Hey, that's great. Now, are you ready for your usual?" He held up two fingers and Chris turned to Ashley. "Are you going to try one of our famous hamburgers?"

"Sounds great," replied Ashley. "I hear they're delicious."

"We think so. Back in a bit." She moved away, joking with a group of patrons at the next table.

"She's a cheerful one." Ashley watched Chris' progress en route back to the kitchen.

"She works at it." Matt spoke quietly. "Her husband was killed last year. Hank was a diver. An experienced one and they never did figure out what went wrong. By the time they got him to the surface, he was gone."

"That's tough." Ashley's thoughts were drawn inexorably back to Paige. "Makes us appreciate every day, huh?"

"Yeah." His eyes lost focus and for a moment he was somewhere else, lost in his own memories. Then his gaze came back to her. "Do you mind if I ask you something?"

Ashley gave a strangled laugh. "I suppose not."

"Where was your husband while all of this was going on, or is that too personal?"

She hesitated and images of her married life scrolled across her mind. She didn't know this man, but he was a good listener, and it felt good to talk freely.

"You're right— it is personal— but for some reason I don't mind telling you." She gave him a tentative smile. "Doug wasn't a bad father." She gave a short, mirthless laugh. "He was an absent father. He's a high-powered lawyer and for the entire time we were together it seemed as though billable hours were more important to him than our marriage. We were never a family unit. The only time we were together as a family was when we went on holidays, and that was only twice during our marriage. He missed Paige's birth and he wasn't there when she died, either." She looked up quickly. "But he was trying an important court case that morning and I had stayed overnight at the hospital so he really couldn't be blamed for that."

He looked at her levelly.

"I suppose it sounds like I'm making excuses for him, but I prefer to think that I've finally accepted him for who he is. It was our love for our daughter that kept us together. Turn on any television talk show or read any self-help book and they'll tell you that's not a good idea, but Paige loved her daddy and at the end I was glad we hadn't separated. He spent a lot of time with her over the last few months of her life and I wouldn't have had it any other way. We grew closer, but not so

much that we wanted to start all over again. That close-
ness made it easier when we filed for divorce." She
looked up and saw understanding in his eyes.

"Here you go." The waitress reappeared with their
burgers and Matt laid some bills on her tray, then stood
to beckon Caitlin.

"You don't have to treat me." Ashley fumbled in her
purse but Chris had disappeared.

Matt caught his daughter's eye then sat back down
again. "Please. I want to. Call it your welcome to
Madrona Island."

Ashley decided to give in graciously. "All right then,
and thank you."

Caitlin appeared at the table, all arms and legs and
appetite. "We saw a hummingbird over there at the
feeder. Do you think it's the same one that comes to our
house?"

Matt frowned, giving her question serious considera-
tion. "I read in our bird book that they're territorial. That
means they choose a certain area and stay there. They
even try to chase other birds away. So no, I don't think
it would be the same one."

Ashley jumped into the conversation. "I saw a Hummingbird this morning at my place. It had a brilliant red
throat."

Caitlin nodded. "That would be a male Rufous Hummingbird. Did you know that the males are brighter
than the females?"

"No I didn't, but I hope I see more. Do they stay here
year-round?"

"Nope." Caitlin was on solid ground now. "They fly

way down South. We also saw a school of fish under the dock and we were trying to catch them with the net but they were too fast."

Matt placed her food in front of her. "That sounds like fun but I don't think you're allowed to take fish that small. Next thing you know I'll be having to bail you out of jail."

Caitlin gave her father an exasperated look. "We know that, Daddy. We were going to put them right back."

"Well that's all right then." Matt winked at Ashley.

Caitlin dunked one of her fries in ketchup and munched on it, eyes closing blissfully. "Did you know that in Holland they eat mayonnaise with their fries?" She licked her fingers, watching for a reaction from Ashley. "That sounds really yucky, if you ask me."

"It takes some getting used to. I was in London a few years ago and we had fries in Regent's Park. They had mayonnaise there too. And vinegar, of course. And ketchup." Paige had been with her and they'd spent a delightful afternoon at the Regent's Park Zoo.

Caitlin nodded thoughtfully. "Did you see Big Ben?"

"Yes I did."

"That's a picture of Big Ben on HP Sauce. On the label. Do you have any children?"

Ashley almost choked on a mouthful of hamburger. Caitlin jumped up and ran to her side, climbing up on the bench and patting her on the back. Her little hand was warm and surprisingly comforting. Matt slid a napkin beneath her hand and she held on to it with clutched fingers. The child sat very close, hand still resting on Ashley's back.

"Are you all right?" Caitlin withdrew her hand but remained close.

Ashley nodded. "I'm fine, thank you." She produced a weak smile. "Choked on a piece of hamburger." The child eyed her own food. "Really," she said gently. "I'm fine. You can finish your lunch now." To prove that she'd recovered she picked up her hamburger and forced herself to take another bite.

"Okay." Caitlin went back to the bench beside her father.

The youngster had evidently forgotten her earlier question because she chatted gaily throughout the remainder of her lunch. Then Matt gave her permission to rejoin her friend and they were once more alone.

"I'm sorry." They spoke the same words, at the same time.

Ashley managed a small smile, but she was exhausted from trying to act as if nothing had happened. "You have nothing to be sorry about," she said, her voice quivering. "I just didn't expect that question—that's all."

Matt nodded his agreement. "I know what you must have been feeling."

"Do you?" She looked at him then. Really looked. And there, beneath the ready smile, was a hint of sadness. She remembered seeing that same look yesterday on the ferry.

Matt took a drink of coffee then stared into the cup. "I had a similar experience, but it was quite a few years ago. We were living on the mainland back then. Emily—that's Caitlin's mother—had made strawberry short-cake for dinner and realized at the last minute that she'd forgotten to buy whipping cream." His voice tightened up. " 'Back in a minute.' That's what she said to me as she jumped on her bike to go to the little corner store a few blocks away. I was sitting out on the front porch with the baby, drinking iced tea, so I heard the sirens right away. I kept telling myself that the reason she hadn't come back was that she was helping someone in some way. She was always putting herself out for other people. That's one of the things I loved about her. But I think that deep down I knew the real reason she hadn't returned. . . . I just didn't want to accept it. Finally I put the baby in the stroller and started to walk toward the store. I got there as the ambulance was leaving and I saw her bike crumpled up on the side of the road. She'd been hit by a young kid in a pickup truck."

He started speaking quickly. "I ran home and put Caitlin into her car seat. I remember that my hands were shaking so much I could scarcely get her buckled in. After that it's a bit of a blur, but I recall the surgeon telling me that her internal injuries were so bad they knew they'd never be able to save her. So they let me sit with her and hold her hand. She opened her eyes once and squeezed my hand. Then she died." He regarded her steadily. "So yes, I do know what it's like to look into the eyes of someone you love and know they're dying." He took a deep breath and gathered himself to continue. "But I didn't tell you all this so we could see who has the saddest story. I told you because I understand." A smile softened his face. "I really do."

Ashley didn't know what to say. A breeze skipped in off the water and she turned her face to it, trying to clear her mind. Movement caught her eye at the end of the adjacent pier and she saw Caitlin and her friend lying on the weathered boards of the dock, peering into the water. She smiled. "You've done a great job raising her, you know."

Matt looked over his shoulder and spotted the two girls. "I like to think so, but today wasn't the first time I've found myself wondering if I encouraged her curiosity a bit too much. I've always told her to ask questions. I figure that I'd rather have her learn things from me than pick up wrong information somewhere else."

Ashley tilted her head sideways, studying him across the table. "What do you do for a living? At first I thought you might be a farmer but your hands are too clean. Besides, farmers don't sit around at the marina during growing season." She hesitated. "At least I don't think they do."

He grinned. "I suspect you're right. No, I'm what my daughter likes to call a computer geek." He seemed content to leave it at that but Ashley was still curious.

"Do you have a special area of expertise?"

"Right now I'm working on software development."

"I wouldn't have thought there's much tech work here on the island."

"That's the good part about my job. I can do a lot of my work from home. I like to be here for Caity."

"I can understand that. They grow up so quickly." She glanced at her watch. "My goodness. It's two thirty. I'm supposed to be meeting my friend Jessica at the three o'clock ferry." She shrugged apologetically. "Sorry to eat and run but she'll never let me live it down if I'm late."

"You should have plenty of time, but if you leave now at least you'll get a parking space fairly close by." He stood up and watched her with a faint grin as she gathered her things. "I'm glad you came, Ashley. It's been nice."

"I'm glad too." And she was. She was intrigued by this quiet man. He exuded an aura of quiet authority that she found surprisingly attractive. For one crazy moment she found herself wishing he would say something about seeing her again, but then she caught herself and looked away. She had no intention of becoming involved with Matt or any other man. Her heart was too raw for emotional entanglements. That was why she'd come here. To be alone. To be quiet. To let her heart heal.

She tossed back her hair and plunked the hat on her head, suddenly self-conscious. She held out her hand. "Thanks again," she murmured, and her hand disappeared in his. The webs at the corners of his eyes deepened as his grin became a full-fledged smile. "I hope you'll be happy here, Ashley. I know we are."

She retrieved her hand and lowered her head, hiding behind the brim of the hat. She was too old to blush, but her body didn't seem to know that. "Thanks again." She chanced a quick look up at him. "Say good-bye to Caitlin from me, will you?"

He nodded and she walked quickly toward the ramp, feeling his eyes on her back. It was just as well he hadn't expressed an interest in seeing her again, because he came with some serious baggage in the form of a daughter. It had been all she could do not to gather

her up in her arms, to inhale the little-girl smell of her, to feel the tangle of arms and legs, and touch the glossy hair.

"I know I'm being irrational," she murmured to herself, "but I can't help it." She slowed at the top of the ramp and looked back down. Caitlin had come back to the picnic table and was up on her knees on the bench, leaning toward her father with a serious expression on her face. They didn't look up and Ashley headed for the van, her mind churning.

"I like her, Daddy." Caitlin sipped the last of her drink. "But she seems awfully sad."

Matt pulled back. It wasn't the first time Caitlin had surprised him with her sensitivity to other people's feelings. It was a bit unnerving, but he'd rather have her this way than wrapped up in herself. "She *is* sad, Caity."

"Why, Daddy?"

He looked into those probing green eyes. "Ashley had a daughter she loved very much." He gave her a squeeze, wondering if he could go on living if he ever lost her. "And she died from a terrible disease." He kept his arm loosely around her shoulders.

Caitlin stayed very still for several long moments. He could tell she was thinking by the tiny movements in her eyes as she absorbed this information. "Does she have a broken heart?" she asked finally, her voice small.

Matt nodded. "Yes, I think that's a good way to describe it." He gave her arm a reassuring squeeze. "Right now I think she's lonely and hurting. She's probably wondering if she'll ever feel better again."

"You mean like Humpty Dumpty." Caitlin looked up at her father. "Remember when I was little and you'd read it to me?" Her eyes grew distant. "All the King's horses and all the King's men / Couldn't put Humpty together again." Matt's heart swelled with love as he watched her, almost as though he knew what her next words would be.

"Maybe we can help her, Daddy. Maybe she's not like Humpty Dumpty after all."

"I hope not, Caity." His gaze drifted up toward the parking lot but the beautiful, fragile woman was long gone. "I hope not."

There was a festive atmosphere at the ferry dock. *Why not?* Ashley thought to herself. *It's a glorious day; people are on vacation and having a good time.* The parking lot slanted down toward the dock. Vehicles filled two lanes, waiting to embark, while the other lane was kept free for arrivals. People wandered among the vehicles and streamed across the open area toward a crowded food kiosk, most individuals leaving with ice cream and cold drinks. A few craft vendors chatted casually with tourists inspecting their wares. None of them seemed concerned about making a sale.

A ripple went through the crowd as the ferry rounded a rocky promontory, followed by an announcement over the loudspeaker that sent most people scurrying for their vehicles. Ashley was left with a few other locals who were meeting people and several walk-on passengers.

As the ferry drew closer she spotted Jessica on the

top deck. Her friend looked wonderful, as usual. Springy hair stood out around her head, a russet halo in the afternoon sun. She wore a bomber jacket of soft leather over a classic T-shirt. Skintight jeans were tucked into tooled cowboy boots, and not for the first time Ashley found herself envying her friend's distinctive style. They had met in seventh grade, when Jessica's family had moved to Vancouver from the prairies. The two girls had bonded immediately, sharing everything from that moment until the present. Jessica was bold in almost every area of her life and Ashley sometimes found herself wondering how they'd remained friends for so many years when they were polar opposites. Or perhaps it was *because* they were different that they got along so well. What she did know was that Jessica would stand by her no matter what. It was a comforting thought.

Long strides brought her friend down the ramp and at five foot nine plus the added height of the cowboy boots, Jessica stood out from most of the other female passengers. She pretended not to recognize Ashley for a moment, then ran back and crushed her in a quick hug. Stepping back, she looked her over, a saucy grin on her face. "Lord, woman. I leave you on your own for two days and you turn into Mother Earth." Her gaze took in the long swirling skirt and straw hat. "I scarcely recognized you."

Ashley relieved her friend of the backpack slung over her shoulder, knowing that Jessica would insist on carrying her own laptop. "Quiet, or I'll make you walk home."

Jessica raised a perfectly shaped brow. "So it's home already? Things are looking up." She strode up the hill toward Ashley's van. "Lead me to it, then."

The two women chatted nonstop on the drive across the island. Ashley pointed out the few landmarks that had become familiar and was soon turning into her new driveway. Jessica's eyes lit up as she caught a glimpse of the ocean and she turned to Ashley, her voice throaty with emotion. "I'm so glad you decided to come here, Ash. It seems like the perfect place for you."

Ashley led the way into the living area and Jessica nodded her approval. "It's just as I imagined it from seeing it online. Except that the pictures didn't do justice to that fabulous deck or the view." Honey trotted out from the sunroom, tail working overtime. Jessica knelt down. "Hello, sweetpea." She looked up at Ashley. "Let's have a drink outside and you can tell me everything that's happened. And don't you dare leave out a thing!"

Jessica dragged one of the lounges into a patch of sun and was removing her cowboy boots when the bald eagle soared by, landing in the dead tree. "I suppose that's the Chamber of Commerce eagle," she said. "If it's trying to impress me, I gotta tell you, it's working." She accepted a glass of iced tea from Ashley and the women watched in reverent silence as the bird pushed off, gliding effortlessly out of sight around the rocky headland.

"A little hummingbird visited me this morning." Ashley frowned. Could that have been just this morning? So much had happened.

"You should put up a feeder. I'll bet you'd have them around here all the time."

"Caitlin told me it's a Rufous Hummingbird."

"Whoa! Who is Caitlin?" Jessica leaned forward, instincts on alert. "You've only been here a day and a half and you already know half the island."

"I was just thinking that it seems much longer than that." Ashley remained silent for a few moments and Jessica waited for her to continue. "And one little girl is hardly half the island. Caitlin is Matt's daughter, and before you ask, he's a man I met on the ferry coming over."

Jessica's eyes widened slightly at the words "little girl" but she was on the scent of something more intriguing. "Don't tell me. I suppose he's a sculptor, or a poet, or maybe he grows rutabagas." She swung her feet onto the deck in order to face her friend. "I warned you, Ash, these islands are populated by artsy-fartsy types or left-over hippies trying to live off the land. Thing is, some of them even make a living. So which is it?"

Ashley shook her head. "You're incorrigible, Jessica Burns. You have to know everything about everyone within five minutes of meeting them."

"Do not!" Jessica grinned. "Ten minutes, tops."

"Yeah, well this may come as a shock to you but not everyone is interview material. By the way, did you finish the story on the Australian prime minister?"

"Yes, I did, and stop trying to change the subject. What does this Matt do for a living? And more important, why are you trying to avoid the question?"

"For heaven's sake, Jess. He's a computer programmer. He's an ordinary guy."

Jessica frowned. "Here? On this island?"

Ashley gestured to her friend's laptop. "You're not the only one who doesn't have to go into the office to work. He's just a local guy trying to make a living, okay? Come on, let's go inside and you can help me make the salad for dinner. We're having steak and a salad."

Jessica watched her friend retreat into the kitchen. She'd leave it alone . . . for now.

After dinner Jessica wandered into the sunroom and stood quietly, arms crossed in front of her chest. "I see you've unpacked the easel." She turned back to her friend. "Does that mean you're thinking of working again?"

Ashley shrugged and continued putting dishes away. "I've been thinking about it. There's some wonderful subject matter around here, and to be honest I think about painting all the time. For example, take that tree out there. I see something like that and I find myself planning what colors I'll use to get the effect I want and how I'll position it in the painting." She looked from Jessica to her brushes. "But that's as far as I've gone. I haven't done any sketches."

"It'll come. Anyway, there's no hurry, is there?"

"Not really." Ashley tried to stay positive. "I talked to Gabrielle a few days ago and she reminded me that she has more than twenty of my paintings and that most of them have never been exhibited. I'd forgotten that when Paige got sick she took down the few that were on display. I didn't think about it at the time, but it was her way of giving me my own space. Anyway, I agreed that she could put them in the next show."

"She's a neat lady." Jessica stifled a yawn. "Do you mind if I make it an early night? I got up early to work on that article and I'm bushed." She gave Ashley a sisterly hug, then stood back, still holding her by the shoulders. "I'm going to miss having you nearby, but I'm glad you're settled here. Besides, you're only a couple of hours away."

"You know it." A lump formed in Ashley's throat. "Now go on and get to bed. See you in the morning."

Ashley was sitting outside the next morning when Jessica wandered out, steaming cup of coffee in hand.

"Why didn't you wake me up?" She absently ruffled Honey's coat.

Ashley looked fondly at her friend. Jessica had always been the one to sleep in and today was nothing new. "Because you were tired. You obviously needed the sleep. Anyway, it's only a little after ten. What time were you going to leave?"

"I was thinking of getting the three o'clock." Jessica sank down on one of the lounges. "It's either that or eight o'clock tonight."

"Is Trevor picking you up?" she asked, referring to Jessica's longtime significant other. Ashley liked his charismatic television personality.

"That's just it. He can pick me up from the three o'clock, but he has to fly to Toronto tonight, so he can't meet me if I take the later ferry. You know, I think that's why we've stayed together for so long. We hardly ever see each other."

"Then you should definitely leave this afternoon." Ashley rose, and Honey was right alongside, tail wagging. "Come on, let's take our coffee down to the beach. I haven't checked it out yet."

Chapter Four

The cove was sheltered and warm. The friends settled on a beached log and Ashley sensed that Jessica was about to say something important.

"Trevor asked me to marry him the other night."

Ashley nodded. "That makes how many times?"

"I dunno—I've lost count. But this was different. It was like he was giving me an ultimatum without actually saying the words."

"Jessica." Ashley chose her words carefully. "Not every marriage is like your parents'. As a matter of fact, most of them are pretty darn good."

Jessica shoved her fingers into the mass of curls crowning her head. "Come on, Ash, you know the statistics. Over fifty percent of marriages end in divorce." Her voice rose. "Fifty percent!"

"Okay, but what about the ones that work? Those

are the ones you should focus on. You love Trevor, don't you?"

"You know I do."

"You're both successful, you work in the same field, and he's crazy about you." She could feel her friend's eyes watching her intently. "Go for it, Jess."

Jessica set down her coffee mug and picked up a handful of pebbles, staring at them blindly. "I heard my parents snipe at each other every day of my life. Even though I was only a kid I knew it shouldn't be that way. It almost tore me apart." She started tossing the pebbles toward the water. "Even you weren't immune. When we were growing up I always thought you'd have the perfect marriage but look what happened."

"Yes, look." Ashley's voice was sharp but she didn't try to temper it. This was too important. "But at least Doug and I tried. And we had the most wonderful little girl. Even knowing the outcome I'd do it all over again."

"I've known you almost my entire life and sometimes I don't understand you." Jessica frowned. "Aren't you bitter? Not even a little bit?"

"Bitter?" Ashley gave her head a slow shake. "I can see why you'd think that, but you know something? Being bitter takes too much energy, too much effort. In the past few years I've put all my energy into holding on to my sanity." She sighed. "Or at least it's seemed that way sometimes. But we're getting off track. We were talking about you and Trevor."

"I'm scared, Ash." Jessica slid a sideways glance at her friend. "Seems unlikely, huh? Jessica Burns being a 'fraidy cat. But I can't put it off forever. He'll be in Toronto for a few days and I'm going to do some serious thinking while he's gone." She let the remaining pebbles slide through her fingers. "Do you think you'll ever marry again?" She waved a hand in the air. "I mean, eventually?"

Ashley threw a stick for Honey and the dog ran after it like a young puppy. "There are times I want that more than anything. When Doug and I first got married and then when we had Paige, I was in seventh heaven." She remained silent for a moment. "I'm not sure I ever told you this, but all I ever wanted was to have a family of my own. I had a good childhood compared with some kids, but I had no siblings and no mother. Dad did his best and I love him, but we weren't like other families. I'd try to imagine what it was like to have brothers and sisters, but I couldn't." Honey dropped the stick beside her and she patted the dog absently. "So yeah, I think about getting married again. But if I ever do, I'll be very choosy and I don't see it happening in the foreseeable future. Right now I just want to be alone for a while."

"I can understand that, and you certainly picked the right place for it." Jessica's attention was drawn to a fishing boat plowing through the channel. It was heading out to the open ocean along with several others in the distance. "Lots of fishing boats heading north." She reached for her coffee mug and cradled it thoughtfully, her eyes on the sparkling ocean. "I've been thinking about doing a piece with a positive spin on the sports fishing industry. Did you know that there are men all over North America—all over the world, really—who pay thousands of dollars to be flown into our remote lakes and rivers? Some women fish too, but it's mainly a guy thing." She jumped up and started to pace back and forth. "It's all catch-and-release, you know. They go back home and spread the word about our unspoiled wilderness areas and the upside is that there's virtually no negative impact on the environment. I need to do something positive once in a while. My environmental pieces are always well received, but researching how we're raping the planet can get downright depressing. This would be a nice change."

Ashley nodded. "I hadn't really thought about what a downer it must be, doing these reports. With me, I just choose a subject that pleases my eye and I go ahead and paint it. But I like your idea of a story about the fishing camps. You can still get your environmental message across but it's more subtle."

"Precisely!" Jessica picked up her mug and drank the last of the coffee. "Come on— let's go back up to the house and I'll make us some French toast for breakfast. That's quick and easy."

"Sounds good to me. I'll set the table."

The doorbell rang as they were finishing breakfast and Ashley looked up, startled. "I wonder who that is?"

"Don't look at me." Jessica gathered up the plates and carried them to the sink. "Why don't you go and find out?"

Ashley relaxed. "Oh, I know who it is. I ordered some flowering planters yesterday and the seller said they'd be delivered today." She headed for the door. "I'll get them to take the planters right out onto the deck."

"Hello Ashley." Matt stood in the doorway, one hand on Caitlin's shoulder.

"Matt." Her mind raced. "How did you find me?" She looked down. "Hello, Caitlin."

He smiled sheepishly. "I asked Brenda Kerr. She didn't want to tell me at first, but I explained that we'd had lunch yesterday and that I had a gift for you." He held up a bag. "So she gave in."

Ashley's eyes went to the bag in his free hand. "Well in that case, please come in."

Honey's tail was wagging furiously and Caitlin ran to her and sat on the floor. The dog jumped up and licked her face.

"Honey, no. Caitlin, you can push her away. She knows she's not supposed to jump on people."

"I don't mind." Caitlin's gaze went from her father to Ashley. "I mean, if it's okay with you."

Ashley laughed. "It's fine with me. She obviously likes you." The sight of the child and the dog together was bittersweet. Paige and Honey had often played in the same way and it was clear that the dog missed her friend.

"Well hello." Jessica came out of the kitchen. She'd dashed into the downstairs bedroom and run a comb through her hair.

"Jessica, this is Matt and Caitlin. Matt, this is my lifelong friend, Jessica Burns."

"How do you do." Matt stepped forward and shook

Jessica's hand. "Caity and I came to bring Ashley a housewarming gift."

"How thoughtful." Jessica eyed the bag. "Hmmm. Home Hardware. What is it, a set of screwdrivers?"

"Sorry, no screwdrivers today." Matt drew out an oddly shaped box wrapped in blue tissue paper. Stars had been stuck on every conceivable surface. It appeared to have been wrapped by someone with only one arm.

"Caitlin insisted on wrapping it up and sticking on the little stars. I told her it wasn't necessary, but I was informed that girls like things like that." Matt seemed embarrassed.

Ashley smiled at the child. "Well, she's right, and I think it's lovely. Shall I open it now?"

"Yes." Three voices spoke at once.

Ashley picked at the Scotch Tape and flattened each piece of tissue as it was removed.

Jessica rolled her eyes and looked at Matt. "She's been like this ever since she was a little girl. She probably still has the paper and the bow from the first birthday present I ever gave her."

"You two have been friends a long time, then."

"Yes, we have. Well, look at that—it's a hummingbird feeder. We were just saying this morning that she needed one."

Ashley smiled up at Matt. "Thank you. And thank you, Caitlin."

"You're welcome." The child looked up from the floor. "It tells you on the side of the box how much sugar to mix in with the water. Don't use that colored stuff. It's not necessary. Can I take Honey outside to the deck?"

"Yes, of course, but don't let her run down to the beach, okay?"

"'Kay."

Matt walked to the slider and looked outside. "You've got a great spot to hang the feeder. Right there, on the branch of the arbutus."

"I'm going to go and mix up some sugar water. Can I offer you a cup of coffee?"

"I'd enjoy that, but only if I'm not interrupting anything." He turned to Jessica. "How long are you staying?"

"I'm afraid I have to go home shortly. I have some research to do on a new story."

"Here, let's sit on these stools by the kitchen counter where we can keep an eye on Caitlin." She found a mug and filled it, then set it down in front of Matt.

"Jessica is an investigative journalist specializing in environmental issues," said Ashley proudly. "Unfortunately she never stays in any one place very long." She looked fondly at her friend.

"There have been some environmental issues here on the island from time to time," mused Matt, "but we manage to deal with them in an equitable manner. The conflicts are usually around logging, quite understandably. No one who owns a home here wants large areas of clear-cut. The other area of concern is development." He laughed shortly. "We all move here because it's unspoiled, and then we object when the next guy wants to move in."

Jessica came right to the point, as usual. "And which

side are you on? Big business or the little guy who wants to keep paradise intact?"

Matt smiled easily. "That's a no-brainer. I'm not against new homes per se, but I'd prefer not to see any more large housing developments. Call me selfish, but I like it here just the way it is."

Jessica nodded, eyes narrowing as she studied him openly. "Can't say I blame you. Where else would you have a bald eagle land so close? Ashley and I saw it yesterday. It seems to like that tree."

Matt turned on the stool and glanced toward the ocean. "Speaking of God's creatures, you're in a perfect area here to spot orcas."

"Here?" Ashley leaned on the other side of the counter. "You really think so?" Her gaze followed Matt's. "I saw a television program recently that talked about the dangers posed by the use of underwater sonar by the military. There are some scientists who think that the use of sonar might cause the orcas to beach, but they can't prove it, of course."

"Now there's an environmental issue." Jessica spoke drily.

"No kidding. I did some follow-up on the Net, and mainly I found out that I have a lot to learn on the subject."

Matt acknowledged her comment with a quick nod. "In this area there are three resident pods. They're referred to as J, K, and L pods. I've been told that it's mostly K pod around here. They range up and down the coast, following the salmon runs."

"I'd love to see them." She turned to Jessica. "You're

the queen of research. What do you consider to be the main concern for their survival?"

"It's their diet. You see, orcas eat salmon. Oh, you see programs on television where they come up on shore after seals and toss them up in the air, but those are in a different area of the world and the images make for some great television." She paused to catch her breath. "But I believe their downfall could come about because of toxins in the food chain. That's something most people can understand. We're pumping waste of all kinds into the ocean at an alarming rate. The little fish are eaten by the bigger fish, and by the time they get to the salmon the poisons are concentrated in their bodies. Then the orcas eat the salmon and bingo! Toxic lunch. The whales in Puget Sound are in real trouble and ours aren't far behind."

"Do I hear the beginnings of a story?" Matt looked at her expectantly.

Jessica shook her head. "No, I don't think so. It's been done a lot recently, but as you can tell I pay close attention." She turned to her friend. "And I'm glad to hear that you've taken an interest too."

Ashley stirred the sugar water and the spoon clinked softly against the glass container. "It's a cause I'd like to get behind. When I'm more settled I think I'll expand my knowledge."

Jessica slid down from the stool. "I hope you guys will excuse me but I haven't even had my morning shower yet and it's almost time to get going." She held out a hand to Matt. "Nice to have met you, Matt. Keep an eye on those orcas for me, will you?"

He stood up. "I surely will."

Jessica disappeared into the back of the house and Ashley was left with Matt. "Thanks again for the feeder," she said, pouring the sugar solution into the bottle. "I know it's going to give me hours of pleasure."

"I'm glad you like it." He followed her out onto the deck. Caitlin and Honey were sitting at the top of the stairs, Caitlin's arm around the dog's neck. The youngster looked up. "I love your dog." She rubbed her face in the dog's coat. "She doesn't smell stinky or anything."

Matt laughed. "One of my sisters lives on a large acreage up in the Okanagan and they have an outside dog."

"Mr. Jiggs," said Caitlin.

Matt continued. "The dog has the run of the place as well as the adjoining farm and he gets into some awful messes."

"I can only imagine," Ashley said with an easy smile. She was surprised at how comfortable she felt with this man.

Matt's gaze lingered on her lips and then he seemed to give himself a little shake. "Come on, Caity, time to go. Ashley's friend has to leave soon."

The child scrambled to her feet and the dog trotted into the house. "Can I come back? I think Honey likes me."

The request took Ashley by surprise. "Well, I don't know. I . . ."

"Caitlin, that's rude. You don't go inviting yourself into people's homes." Matt's tone was gentle.

"Why not, Daddy?" She looked from her father to Ashley.

Matt chuckled. "For one thing, it's considered impolite. You're supposed to wait until you're asked."

"In that case, I invite you." The words popped out before Ashley realized it. "You can come by anytime."

"There, see, Daddy?" She followed Honey into the sunroom, where she'd curled up in her basket. "I'll come and see you again, Honey, so you won't be too lonely."

Matt followed her into the room. "Time to go, sweetie." His tone was much firmer this time. Caitlin gave the dog one last pat and then ran toward the door.

Matt stopped beside the easel, his eyes questioning. "Do you paint?"

Ashley was glad that most of her supplies were still boxed up. She wanted him to like her for herself, not because she had gained a reputation as a painter. Her thoughts startled her and she flushed. "I might try a few paintings while I'm here." She lowered her eyes. "I haven't really felt like it recently."

"Uh-huh." He looked once more then followed Caitlin down the hall. "Thanks for the coffee."

"You're welcome. And thank you for the feeder." A dark green Land Rover sat in the roundabout. Caitlin had already climbed in.

Ashley hadn't pegged him as the Land Rover type. "Where's the truck?"

"We use it mostly for hauling stuff around." He climbed into the driver's seat and gave her a long look. "I hope you get lots of hummingbirds and that you like living here."

Ashley's reply was cut off by the arrival of Don from

the nursery. He jumped out of the delivery van, waved at Matt, then turned to Ashley. "Where would you like the planters?"

"Could you take them around to the front deck, please?"

"Be glad to." He lowered a ramp and wheeled the first one down on a dolly, disappearing around the side of the house.

"I'll be off, then." Matt waved out the window and Caitlin's little arm appeared on the passenger side. Ashley watched the SUV climb up to road level, and the day lost some of its brightness. She was glad for the distraction when Don came back with the dolly, whistling tunelessly.

"You know Matt, then?" He strode up the ramp and loaded the second planter.

"Not really." Was this normal island behavior? Questioning people about who they knew? "I met him a couple of days ago when I came over on the ferry."

He gave her a startled look. "He was on the ferry?"

"Yes." She was becoming irritated. "He was bringing a bike for his daughter."

"Oh." He rolled the planter along the walkway and she followed him to the deck.

Flowers cascaded over the sides of the planters, adding vibrant splashes of color to the deck. "They're just what I wanted," she said. "Thank you very much."

"You're welcome." He made his way back to the van, closed up the back, and was headed up the driveway before she could ask him what he'd been getting at. She wandered slowly back into the house and gathered up the coffee mugs, placing them in the sink. There'd be plenty of time to wash them when she got back.

"Now that's more like it." Jessica spotted the planters on the deck. "I thought I heard something while I was in the shower."

"Yes, and Matt and Caitlin left too."

"Good."

"Good? Why do you say that?" Sometimes it was hard to follow Jessica's train of thought.

"Because I can't ask you about him if he's here." Jessica flicked her fingers. "Come on, give."

There was no sense trying to hold back. Her friend would only worm it all out of her eventually. She took a deep breath. "Jess, I've already told you everything. I met him on the ferry on Friday and I saw him at the farmers' market on Saturday. Caitlin grows vegetables and sells them at the market. He invited me for lunch and I met them later at the marina."

"You see!" Jessica pointed a finger. "You didn't tell me that before. I was thinking about him in the shower and I didn't think you'd told me about meeting his daughter."

"I had lunch with him, okay?" Ashley was getting defensive. "Why are you giving me the third degree, anyway?"

"Hello. Earth to Ashley. The man is gorgeous." She peered at her friend. "Come on, Ash, you've got to admit it—on a scale of one to ten, he's . . . he's off the scale."

"He's okay, I guess."

"He's more than okay. Take my word for it." She

hummed a little tune and Ashley could tell she was thinking. "Why do you think he lives here?"

"Gee, Jess, I don't know. Maybe he likes it." She rolled her eyes.

Jessica waved the explanation away. "Yeah, but I feel like I'm missing something. Like I should know him. Is he divorced? What's his last name?"

"I have no idea. Will you stop with the questions?" Ashley looked at the clock. "Shouldn't we get going?"

Jessica gathered up her laptop and her overnight bag and they climbed into the van. The journalist drummed her fingers on the outside of her laptop. "What if I do some research on him?"

"No. Absolutely not." She realized she'd have to give her friend a bit more. "He's not divorced. His wife died when Caitlin was very small. I don't want to know anything else about him, Jess, I really don't. I just want to live a quiet life here on the island and do my own thing."

Jessica held up her hands. "Okay, okay. I admit I get carried away sometimes." She shot Ashley a sly look. "But he *is* a hunk."

Ashley couldn't help but smile. "Okay, he's a hunk." If only Jessica knew that she'd woken this morning thinking of eyes the color of lapis lazuli. But she couldn't tell her that. She could scarcely admit it to herself.

Ashley raised a hand as the ferry pulled out. Jessica was at the rail on the lower deck, and acknowledged with a wave of her own, then turned and headed toward the coffee shop, her steps long and confident on the moving deck.

It would be good to get home where it was quiet. The thought sneaked up on Ashley as she walked slowly back to the car. She loved Jessica's company and her whirl-wind personality, but sometimes it could be tiring. For a moment she sat in the car, her mind drifting, touching on everything that had happened since she'd first arrived on the island. It had been a full, busy weekend and she'd en-joyed it, but it was time to slow down. She turned the key in the ignition and pulled onto the almost-deserted road. A thicket of wild roses bordered the road for a few hun-dred yards and she inhaled the soft, evocative scent. Paige had discovered a patch of wild roses one summer and had insisted on collecting a bouquet for her mother, thorns and all. Ashley smiled, the memory clutching at her heart. As she turned the key in the door, Honey ran down the hallway, nails scrabbling on the laminate floor. Ashley picked her up, holding the small warm body to her chest. Honey had been devoted to Paige, and seeing her with Caitlin this weekend had brought back so many memories. Lost in thought, she wandered into the sun-room, put down the dog, and slid onto the stool in front of the easel. Then she raised her eyes and looked beyond the windows. Late afternoon had always been her fa-vorite time of day. The sun was at its warmest, imbuing even the most ordinary scene with rich, golden tones. Watching the lengthening shadows a faint smile played across her lips. With the passing of every hour she was more at peace, and it felt good.

Chapter Five

The ring tone of her cell phone shattered her reverie and she flipped it open.

"Gabrielle." She greeted the gallery owner with a smile in her voice. "Great to hear from you."

"I've been thinking about you, *ma petite*," the French-woman said. "I hope you don't mind my calling so soon."

"Not at all." Ashley walked out onto the deck. "I'm all settled in and the house is everything I hoped it would be. Right now I'm watching several sailboats. No wonder so many writers and artists come here for inspiration."

"*Bien*. I'm glad you like it." Gabrielle paused and Ashley could hear the flick of a cigarette lighter followed by a deep inhalation. "I'm . . . how you say . . . killing two birds with one stone. Since we're displaying your work I wanted to remind you about the summer show and see if you've changed your mind about attending."

"That's coming up in a couple of weeks, isn't it? Where has the time gone?" Ashley stilled as a hummingbird darted up to the feeder then sped off just as quickly. "I'm not sure if I'm ready, Gabby."

"*J'entends.* I understand." Ashley could imagine her friend waving the cigarette in the air. "I won't bother you again, but if you decide to come, let me know and I'll arrange a hotel room for you. I've had quite a few patrons asking why I have none of your paintings in the gallery right now but they all agreed to wait for the show. There's a lot of interest in your work, but that's nothing new." The Frenchwoman's voice became brisk. "If you decide to come let me know if I can be of help—or if you prefer, just show up. Either way, you know I'd be happy to see you."

"Thanks, Gabrielle. And thank you for being so understanding."

For several long moments after the call ended she gazed into the distance. Although she usually enjoyed attending shows and hearing feedback on her work, she wasn't sure if she was ready to put herself out there. A sense of peace settled over her and she sat down on the top step of the deck to watch the sun move inexorably toward the horizon. All in good time.

Ashley couldn't remember the last time she'd been truly alone. At first she felt guilty for focusing on herself but guilt gave way to acceptance and parts of her soul that she thought had dried up and died began to come back to life. Tuning in to the rhythms of the island, she found herself following the path of the sun, watching the play of light and shadow in the surrounding trees. Some days she did nothing but relax on a chaise lounge with a book. Or she was content to sit on the top step of the stairs leading down to the beach, absorbing the tidal patterns and the sound of waves breaking on the small beach. Many hummingbirds had discovered her feeder and she observed that they ceased their territorial squabbling just before dark, when for a few minutes they cooperated, sharing the nectar prior to settling down for the night.

Her only personal contact was with the clerk at the grocery store when she went to buy groceries midweek. And with Jessica, who called to say that she had agreed to marry Trevor and that the wedding would take place in the fall. Even her normally ebullient friend seemed to sense that she needed her space, and kept her calls brief.

With a sense of relief she realized that her sleep patterns began to normalize. Fresh air and zero stress brought long nights of healing sleep and her energy level started to climb.

"All right Honey, you've been patient long enough. We're going beachcombing." The dog wagged her tail as though understanding every word. The Weather Channel promised another sunny day and based on her observations of the tides, Ashley knew without checking that her small beach would be exposed for a few hours this morning.

"Now let me think. What do I want to take?" She plunked the straw hat on her head and grabbed a large fabric purse. "Water, sunglasses, binoculars, and maybe some sunscreen. Just in case." She gathered the items and tossed them into the voluminous purse alongside her ever-present sketch pad.

"Ready?" She stepped out onto the deck and was about to close the slider when the doorbell rang. Who could be bothering her at this time of day? She considered ignoring it, but that didn't seem like a neighborly gesture on such a small island.

"Hello." Caitlin stood proudly in the sunshine, her bicycle propped against the side of the house. "I came to visit you." Eager eyes looked beyond Ashley and lit up when she spotted Honey running down the hallway. "You said it would be all right."

"Well, yes . . . of course." Ashley looked hopefully up the driveway, but she knew she wouldn't see the Land Rover. "Did you ride over here all by yourself?" It was a silly question; the child was obviously alone. "Honey and I were just about to go down to the beach. Would you like to come with us?"

"Yes, please." The child knelt down and whispered to the squirming dog. "You'd like that, wouldn't you?" The dog danced backward and gave a soft *woof* of agreement.

"Did you tell someone where you were going?" Ashley recalled Matt's earlier admonition to his daughter.

Caitlin stood up, nodding vigorously. "I told Mrs. Archibald."

Ashley pictured the child confiding in her goldfish. "Who's Mrs. Archibald?" she asked. She hated to pry, but it was important.

"Our housekeeper." Caitlin walked down the hallway, fondling the dog's ears. "She told me to ride carefully."

Ashley was taken aback. Matt hadn't seemed like the kind of man who could afford a housekeeper. "Perhaps we should give her a call and tell her where you are." She picked up her cell phone from the counter. "What's the number?"

Caitlin gave her a long look. "Daddy doesn't like me to give out the phone number, but I guess it's okay." She dropped her eyes. "He says he likes his privacy."

Ashley could relate to that. "I don't blame him." She handed the phone to the child. "You go ahead and phone. I don't need to know the number."

Caitlin dialed, spoke with someone on the other end, then handed the phone to Ashley. "She wants to talk to you."

"Hello there." The woman's voice was warm and motherly. Ashley pictured her pulling a batch of cookies from the oven. "I hope you don't mind our Caitlin dropping in on you like that, but Matthew told me it was fine with him if it was okay with you. The child has been wanting to visit you for days now, but her father made her wait."

Ashley was grateful for Matt's sensitivity. "No, I don't mind at all. We're on our way down to the beach."

"Well, I won't keep you then. But if you don't mind, would you call me after she leaves?"

"I'd be happy to." Ashley had already taken note of the number on the display. "It's Mrs. Archibald, is it?"

"Aye. Archie and I take care of Mr. Matthew and the little one. Right, then. Have a good time at the beach."

Caitlin was bursting with information as they made their way down the steep stairs and onto the beach.

Much of it centered on bicycle excursions she had taken with her friend Kimberly to various spots on the island. ". . . and we found a secret spot on East Side Road where nobody else ever goes." Her eyes sparkled with excitement. "We pretend it's our own little island and we're survivors of a terrible shipwreck and the pirates are after us. Oh, look at the shell." She ran to the water's edge and dug around a partly submerged shell, easing it out of the sand. "Too bad," she said, her face clouded by disappointment. "It's broken." She handed the piece to Ashley. "Shall I look for a better one? I'll bet I can find a better one for you." Without waiting for an answer she ran off, Honey bounding along at her heels.

"Don't go too close to the water," Ashley called after the retreating figure.

"Okay." The child turned and waved while the ecstatic dog bounded around her feet.

Ashley settled herself above the high-tide mark, her back to a large piece of driftwood. Caitlin and the dog had made their way to the far end of the beach where layered shelves of sandstone trapped small pools of tidal water. Caitlin crouched down beside one of the pools, staring intently into its depths, one arm around Honey.

Without taking her eyes from the two figures, Ashley reached for her purse. The scene couldn't have been more perfect if she'd posed it herself. Her fingers closed over her sketch pad and she pulled it out, relieved to see that her favorite pencil was still clipped to the spine. With quick, sure strokes she sketched the idyllic scene, making notes around the margins in her own personal shorthand. The sketch was completed before she was aware of what she had done. She studied it for a moment and smiled. She would paint this scene. Maybe not today, but soon. The knowledge gave her a warm glow of contentment and she closed her eyes, lulled by the warmth of the sun and the soothing sound of waves in the sheltered bay.

"Are you asleep?"

Ashley clawed her way up from the depths of a deep, dreamless sleep. Caitlin stood above her, blocking out the sun.

"Not anymore." Ashley picked up the sketch pad, which had slid off her lap and patted the coarse sand beside her. "Would you like to sit down?"

"Yes, please."

Caitlin sat down beside her, snuggling into the warmth of her side. The feel of the child's body was achingly familiar and Ashley forced herself to stay relaxed.

"What's this?" asked Caitlin, picking up the sketchbook. "Can I look?"

Ashley nodded, unsure if she could find her voice.

The child studied the sketch and darted a quick glance up at Ashley. "That's me," she said after a moment. "And Honey." She handed it back to Ashley and squirmed around until she faced her. "Daddy said you had a daughter, and she died." Wind swirled around within the semicircle of the bay, blowing the child's hair into her face. She brushed it aside unconsciously, green eyes fixed on Ashley. "You must miss her a lot."

Ashley shut her eyes and waited for the gut-wrenching pain that slammed into her every time she talked about Paige. She braced herself, but it didn't come. Tempered by time and eased by the soothing pace of life on the island, it had become a throbbing loss somewhere down deep in her soul. It would always be with her, but she could live with it. She opened her eyes and glanced down at the sketch. In a way it was proof that she'd soon be getting on with her life.

"Yes," she found herself saying, her voice a rasping whisper. "I do." The words were surprisingly calming, and her erratic heartbeat went back to normal.

The child nodded. "I told Daddy that you have a Humpty Dumpty heart."

"A Humpty Dumpty heart," Ashley repeated and found herself smiling. "I suppose you're right. I never quite thought of it that way." She tucked the sketch pad in her bag. "I just know that I miss my daughter every day." It felt good to admit it.

Caitlin looked up at Ashley, studying her features. "I think Daddy misses my mom too." A small frown creased her forehead. "I wish I could remember her, but I don't. I was just a baby when she died." She'd been stroking Honey and her hand stilled. "Will you take care of my Daddy while I'm away at camp?"

"Camp?" she repeated, startled by the rapid change in subject. By now she should be used to the way the girl's mind darted around. "That will be fun."

"Yes, but not if I'm worried about my daddy." The child frowned, then settled back in the crook of Ashley's arm. "He'll miss me."

"I'm sure he will, Caitlin, but I really don't think he needs me to take care of him." She found herself smiling again, and gave the girl's shoulders a gentle squeeze.

"But if it makes you feel better I'll check on him while you're gone and see how he's doing."

"Thank you." The child sighed and looked out over the sparkling water. "Do you have any ice cream?"

"As a matter of fact, I do." Ashley closed the sketch pad and stuffed it in her bag. "Come on, let's go get some."

They sat side by side at the top of the stairs and ate their ice cream. Caitlin put down her empty bowl and stuck a hand in the pocket of her shorts, bringing out a handful of shell fragments. "Do you think I could make a necklace out of shells if I got some more?" She pushed them around with her finger. "I'd like to make one for Kimberly for her birthday."

"Hmmm." Ashley studied the shells. "You'd have to ask your Dad to drill holes in them. I'm not sure how easy that would be." She picked one up and turned it over. "How soon is your friend's birthday?"

"It's not until next month but it's going to be a lot of work, so I thought I should get started."

"You're right about that." Ashley chuckled and made a snap decision. For the past few days she'd been toying with the idea of attending the art show in Vancouver, and Caitlin's comment helped her to make up her mind. She'd attend the art show after all. And while she was there, she'd buy something for Caitlin.

"You know, I'll be going to Vancouver this weekend and I know a bead shop. I'm sure they'll have some shells. I'd be happy to bring you enough to make a necklace. Would you like that?"

Caitlin hesitated, but Ashley could see that the idea excited her. "I think so, but I'll have to check with my daddy first." She lowered her eyes. "I'm not allowed to take gifts from people."

"That's very wise, but maybe you could ask him about it and give me a call."

The relief in the child's eyes was immediate. "Okay, I'll call you as soon as I ask him." She checked her watch. "I'd better get going. Daddy said he might be home early tonight."

Caitlin turned and waved at the top of the driveway. Ashley stood and watched the spot for a few minutes after she'd gone, aware of a warm feeling in her heart. Then, remembering her promise, she called Mrs. Archibald.

"Hello?" Matt answered, and her heart did a little tap dance.

"Oh." She fumbled with the phone, almost dropping it. "I didn't expect you to answer."

"Ashley." His voice was like liquid velvet. Her legs were inexplicably weak and she slid onto a stool for support. "I hear Caitlin has been visiting you. I apologize for not having her call you first, but I didn't know your number."

She wondered if that was his way of asking for her number, and if his eyes were as blue as she remembered, and if she was imagining the attraction that sizzled between them like summer lightning. There was a pause on the other end of the line.

"Ashley? Are you still there?"

"Sorry." What had he been saying? She couldn't remember. It must have been something about Caitlin. "We had a good visit. We went down to the beach and I did a sketch."

"That's good, isn't it?" His voice had softened.

In the future she'd have to watch herself around him. He seemed to be able to draw out her most private thoughts and emotions.

"Yes, it is." It also felt right to be sharing the breakthrough with him. "A small step, but it's one in the right direction."

"Good. Will we be seeing you at the market this weekend?" There was a moment's hesitation in his voice. "I was hoping we could have lunch together again."

For a moment she was tempted to change her mind about the Vancouver trip, but she'd promised to buy the shells for Caitlin. "I'm sorry but I can't." The disappointment in her voice was genuine. "I'm going to Vancouver this weekend."

"That's good." He gave a low, sensual chuckle. "Well, not for me, of course, but I'd like to think there will be other weekends." He paused. "There *will* be other weekends, won't there?"

"Oh yeah," she was glad he was on the other end of the telephone and couldn't see her blush. "There'll be other weekends."

"Then I'll let you go. Have a good time."

The island faded into the distance and she turned her attention toward the skyline of Vancouver, surprised at how quickly she'd become accustomed to the unhurried pace of island life. She couldn't imagine plunging back into that hectic lifestyle. Honey would miss her while she was gone, but Gloria had promised to check on her twice a day and at least the dog was in familiar surroundings. She'd been forced to put Honey in a kennel once and the dog hadn't eaten for almost a week. Shuddering at the memory, she turned her thoughts to the exhibition, which started tonight.

But first things first. She hadn't bought any new clothes for what seemed like forever, and she'd taken the morning ferry to give herself plenty of time to visit her favorite clothing store in Park Lane Mall. At least it used to be her favorite store. . . . She wondered if they'd even remember her after all this time.

"Mrs. Stewart, how nice to see you again." Her favorite saleslady greeted her warmly.

"Hello, Leah. How's that new grandson of yours?"

"Growing like the proverbial weed. He'll be starting kindergarten this fall." The woman beamed.

Had it really been that long? The last time she'd been in the store Leah had been puffed up with pride that her grandson had taken his first steps. But that was before—

"However, I'm sure you didn't come in to talk about my grandson."

Ashley was grateful for the change in subject. "I was hoping to find something to wear to a cocktail party tonight." She paused. There wouldn't be much call for a cocktail dress on the island. "Nothing too elegant. More on the informal side. Soft and flowing, if you have anything like that."

"I know just the dress for you. It came in yesterday and it's still in the back." She guided Ashley to the long dresses. "In the meantime, you might like to look these over."

Ashley looked through the dresses. They were lovely, but none were what she wanted. So when Leah reappeared with the dress on a hanger, one arm holding it up from the floor, she gasped with delight.

"Now, that's more like it." The fabric, in rich, dark lavender, was soft and sensuous. It reminded her of the first time she'd seen a Japanese iris, its broad petals vividly splashed with color. "I think I'll try it on."

Demure when viewed from the front, the dress had a halter top and fitted bodice. The skirt fell away in layers and flowed sinuously as she walked to the mirror. Bare in the back, the dress skimmed over her waist and hips, then flared slightly at the hem. Ashley didn't have to be told that she looked good. As a matter of fact, she looked downright sexy and for the first time since she and Doug had separated she longed for some male company. What was Matt doing right now? She gave a small pirouette and the skirt swirled enticingly. Would he like it?

She scowled at the image in the mirror. She couldn't keep thinking about him like this, wondering what he was doing, what he would think. Was she becoming involved with him too quickly? It was something to consider, but not right now. She turned to Leah. "What do you think?"

"It's perfect." The saleswoman eyed her critically. "You've lost a bit of weight, but it suits you. And the dress is the perfect length."

Ashley shivered, and goosebumps popped up along her forearms.

"What you need is a stole to go with that." The saleswoman ducked behind a counter. "There's a silk screening studio on the North Shore and I've been bringing in some of their things." She unfolded a length of shimmering silk and Ashley gasped. Jewel tones of amethyst and sapphire, along with touches of the palest pink blended together artfully. The effect was stunning against the dress and she knew at once that it was perfect.

"May I make a suggestion?" Leah walked back toward the display case. "Do you ever wear dangly earrings?"

Ashley hesitated. "Not for a long time, but I've gone this far so let's have a look."

"These earrings look like they were made to go with that outfit." She held up a pair of beaded earrings. An elongated diamond shape had been crafted out of tiny amethyst crystals.

Ashley held them up to her ears, admiring the way they sparkled and danced with the movement of her head. "You're right. They're just what I need."

Chapter Six

"Do you have shoes and a bag to go with this?" inquired the saleswoman as she wrapped Ashley's purchases.

"No, but I'll stop at that shoe store at the other end of the mall. I've had luck there before." Ashley couldn't stop grinning. "Thanks a lot."

Humming to herself, she wandered along in the mall, swinging the shopping bag. The bead store was on the way to the shoe store, and she stopped in, explained her needs, and left half an hour later with a bag of supplies.

"Your room is ready, Mrs. Stewart." The room clerk handed her the key. "The bellman will help you with your bags."

"Thank you." She followed the bellman up to the room and stood looking out the window long after he'd left. It was unsettling to look out on Vancouver from a

hotel room. She'd grown up here and had always considered it "her" town, but she acknowledged that she'd
also begun to feel that she belonged on the island. She
allowed her thoughts to wander across the water to her
new home . . . to the relaxed way of life . . . to a man
with hair the color of ripe wheat and eyes that made her
heart beat faster every time she looked in them.

With a soft snort of annoyance she forced herself to
focus on the scenery. Lions Gate Bridge dominated the
skyline to the left, an elegant connection to Stanley Park
and the downtown area. Headlights sparkled on the
bridge, flowing like a string of iridescent beads as com-
muters made their way home, and she smiled to herself.
There was no reason she couldn't live in both worlds.
She turned away from the window and started to lay out
her new purchases. She might be attending the show
alone, but she'd look great doing it! She gave her outfit
one last satisfied look and went to draw a bath.

The young female concierge smiled as Ashley exited
the elevator and made her way across the lobby. They
had talked earlier about the dress store, agreeing that
they stocked a tempting range of garments.

"Taxi, ma'am?" Ashley nodded and the doorman
beckoned one of the taxis out of the rank that stood waiting. She couldn't help but notice the flare of appreciation
in the young man's eyes; she felt like Cinderella going to
the ball.

On the short drive to the gallery Ashley wondered
how she'd react when she saw the familiar building. In
her mind the gallery was connected with happier times,

and she hadn't seen Gabrielle in person for well over a year . . . closer to two. But she needn't have worried. Many years ago the building had been a gracious old home. Now light spilled from the windows, and the new canopy Gabrielle had installed a few years ago sparkled with mini-lights. As she exited the taxi, the gentle sounds of Bach wafted from the open windows. Patrons wandered from room to room, champagne flutes in hand as they made their way through the crowd.

Ashley was happy for Gabrielle. Mounting a show was a lot of work, something most people did not appreciate. Gabrielle's evenings were always first class, with drinks and appetizers provided by one of the North Shore's trendiest caterers. She also produced a printed catalogue of the works on display. The gallery attracted an eclectic mix of young professionals, old "establishment" collectors and those who simply enjoyed seeing what was new and exciting.

Ashley was glad to be back in the familiar building. The former residence lent itself well to displaying different artists in the four large downstairs rooms. She was familiar with only one of the other artists being featured tonight, but was pleased to see that red dots denoting "sold" adorned many of the paintings. In many ways it didn't seem that long ago that she'd experienced the thrill of selling her first painting.

Gabrielle caught her eye across the room and raised an elegant eyebrow. She was speaking with an older couple, and Ashley assumed that they were serious buyers because the gallery owner made no effort to slip away from them. She spoke to one of the servers and a tall glass of bubbly liquid appeared in front of Ashley moments later. It was one of the things they had bonded over—their mutual aversion to alcohol. Ginger ale was close enough to champagne that no one noticed, and as Ashley raised her glass to drink, Gabrielle saluted her with her own glass.

A newspaper reporter spotted Ashley and greeted her effusively. He'd always been a bit too pompous for her liking, but he'd interviewed her twice before and had been accurate and fair in his reporting—she had to respect him for that. He chatted away and after a few moments she realized that he had no idea that she'd been out of circulation. Relaxing, she let her gaze drift over the crowd, relieved when the reporter spotted someone else he "just had to talk to."

Free to wander, she supposed she should make an effort to locate her own paintings, which were probably in the far room. Although the rooms flowed into one another, Gabrielle had managed to make the largest room seem special. The lighting was more dramatic, and customers had to walk down two very broad steps into what was now a distinctive sunken gallery. That had been another banner day for Ashley—when her work had first been shown in that room. She could still remember seeing one of her paintings professionally lit for the first time. It had seemed like a dream and for a moment she'd doubted that it was one of hers, but of course the A. STEWART in small letters in the bottom right-hand corner confirmed that she was wide-awake. That moment had imbued her with confidence and she'd begun to believe in her dreams of becoming a professional painter. She'd worked too hard to gain recognition to give it all up now. She turned away from the wall and found Gabrielle making her way through the crowd.

"Ashley!" The Frenchwoman kissed her on both cheeks. "I'm so glad you decided to come." She pulled back and studied Ashley's face, which evidently passed inspection. "Your room. It's all right, *non*?"

"Of course, Gabby. It's wonderful." She leaned closer to the older woman. "It looks like things are going well tonight."

"Yes, well . . ." She looked around, dark eyes pausing at each red dot as she scanned the artwork on the walls. "The new artists are selling well. I am happy for them."

"I was just thinking about the first time I saw one of my paintings on the wall." She shook her head. "Seems like such a long time ago."

Gabrielle glanced around the room then lowered her voice. "You look wonderful, *chérie*. You are well?" From the beginning, Gabrielle had been attuned to her moods. It sometimes seemed as though Gabrielle could read her mind.

"Yes, thanks. Moving to the island has been so good for me." She hesitated, then decided to plunge right in. "I'm going to start painting again next week. I've already decided on the subject matter."

"Bien." Gabrielle nodded emphatically. "You already know that I can sell anything you produce. Customers have been asking about your work for some time now. But I told you about that already, didn't I?" She answered her own question. "Yes, I did. As a matter of fact, there is a gentleman"—she managed to scan the room without appearing obvious—"who was asking if you would be

here tonight. I don't see him right now, but he already owns one of your paintings and has been looking at *Distant Thunder*."

Ashley's eyes widened. "He must have deep pockets." She had been startled at the valuation Gabrielle had arrived at for the painting. It was a large canvas, but even so the price had taken her breath away.

"You could say that." The gallery owner paused to answer a question from her assistant then turned back to Ashley. "Duty calls," she said soberly, but her eyes were gleaming. "Someone wants to buy another painting."

Ashley watched the small, elegant figure weave her way through the crowd. Gabrielle was a true saleswoman, something she would never be. Thanks to Gabby's acute business sense, Ashley didn't care if *Distant Thunder* sold tonight or not. She would be financially independent for the rest of her life.

She set her glass down on the tray of a passing waiter and wandered through the gallery, heading toward the sunken room. There was a good crowd for a Friday night and she had no doubt that the rest of the weekend would continue to be busy as well.

She paused at the steps leading down to the last gallery, where her paintings were displayed. Gabrielle had created an intimate atmosphere with minimal overhead lighting, using track lighting to illuminate Ashley's paintings. They glowed on the walls and she let her gaze run over them, reacquainting herself with work that had been completed more than four years ago. A young couple studied one of the canvases on her left, heads together. Experiencing an unaccustomed jolt of envy, Ashley tore her eyes away and silently entered the room, pausing at the bottom of the stairs.

At the back of the narrow room, a tall man was silhouetted against the glow of the lights. Standing very still, he was studying one of her paintings with an intensity that was palpable. He wore a dark, beautifully cut suit. Doug had been an impeccable dresser, and Ashley had once joked to Jessica that she could spot a bespoke suit across a ballroom, but this was different. This suit took custom-tailoring to a new level, subtly emphasizing the man's broad shoulders and long legs. It fit him better than any suit Doug had ever possessed. The man moved, tilting his head fractionally, and she sensed that he had come to a decision. Her gaze moved past him to the painting on the wall.

He was examining *Distant Thunder*. Ashley didn't usually name her paintings, but Gabrielle had insisted that this one deserved such an honor and had ordered a small engraved plaque, which was attached to the frame. She could remember the day the painting had been conceived as if it were yesterday.

They had been driving across the prairies to attend the wedding of Doug's younger sister in Winnipeg, and somewhere in central Saskatchewan they'd turned off the Trans-Canada Highway for a break from the monotony of endless miles of straight road. Ashley recalled how her entire body had relaxed as they slowed down, how she'd been captivated by the gentle undulations of the prairie. It had been that special time of day when the harsh, unrelenting sun was giving way to the golden light that often precedes a prairie dusk. On a small rise in the road the scene in the painting unrolled before them and Ashley asked Doug to stop the car. Paige had been reading and stayed in the car with Doug, but Ashley had jumped out and taken several pictures in an effort to capture the ethereal glow. It shimmered around her like a cloud of golden fairy dust and her senses thrilled with the beauty of it. She stood by the side of the road, mute, absorbing the scene, imprinting the colors, textures and yes, even the sounds, on her memory.

A weathered rail fence snaked along the edge of the road, then took a turn to the east, skirting the sea of ripe wheat. The wheat glowed, stalks bending in unison as an invisible giant hand brushed the heat from the land. Perhaps disturbed by the breeze, a hawk rose effortlessly from a nearby telephone pole and Ashley followed its flight until it disappeared into a small valley. She had been so busy absorbing the contrast between the old fence and the grain that she hadn't noticed the roiling thunderheads in the distance. She watched them march across the distant hills, dark and ominous. Closer to the horizon, rain slanted down, backlit by jagged slashes of lightning. On the wind the distinctive smell of ozone wafted toward them.

It had been one of the last trips they had taken as a family.

Ashley took a few more steps into the room, noticing that many of the paintings sported red dots. Even more reason why she should start painting again.

She was alone in the room now, except for the man at

the end. He moved closer to the painting, stepping into the light. His hair glowed and for one crazy moment she caught her breath, thinking that it was Matt. But it couldn't be. . . . He was on the island, probably helping Caitlin get ready for the market tomorrow morning. Besides, to be practical, she had no idea if Matt could afford one of her paintings. She decided to approach the man. They were alone in the room, and if he wanted to meet the artist, what better time than now?

"Hello." She spoke softly, not wanting to startle him.

The man turned slowly, as if in a trance, the expression on his face a mixture of surprise and delight. "Ashley. What are you doing here?" It was Matt.

Her mouth opened, but no sound came out. It was the same man, but it wasn't. This man was urbane, confident, and devastatingly handsome. She was so delighted to see him that she couldn't hold back a broad smile.

He took a step toward her. "You look . . ." His eyes were sending her signals before he formed the words. "You look wonderful." Taking her hand he twirled her around, his eyes reflecting his appreciation of her outfit. Her knees wobbled and she had to concentrate to remain standing.

"What are you doing here?" he asked again. "I mean, I'm delighted to see you, but what a coincidence." He gestured around the room. "Are you a friend of Gabrielle's, a customer . . . what?"

"Yes," she said, intentionally vague, teasing him with a smile. "But what about you? What on earth are you doing here? Are you . . ." Her hand flew to her mouth. "Are you the man who's been looking at *Distant Thunder*?"

The instant the words were out of her mouth she regretted them. Why had she embarrassed him by suggesting that he was interested in buying the painting?

"Yes, I am." He didn't seem to think her question unusual. He glanced down at the catalogue in his hand. "I have a previous work by this artist and it's given me a great deal of pleasure."

Ashley was stunned. She could feel a blush creeping up her neck but thankfully he didn't notice in the low lighting. She turned back toward the painting. "So tell me what you like about this one."

"That's easy." He placed a hand at the small of her back and drew her toward the painting. His touch was electric and she had trouble concentrating on his next words.

"I know this place."

Startled, she gave him a sideways glance. "You do?"

"Well, maybe not this precise spot." He dropped his hand and she ached to grab it and put it back. "What I mean is that I've been in places like it. I know what the artist was trying to convey with this painting. I can smell the prairie air. It's heavy with the coming rain, and there's a slight breeze in the air." He gestured toward the painting with the catalogue. "See here? See how he's managed to capture the way the wheat changes color when the wind disturbs it? I feel as though I could take a walk in that wheat field. That's how real it seems to me." He turned to her with a boyish grin. "So, do you think I should buy it?"

"Matt, you're asking the wrong person." She should

have told him right away. She hated to have him think that she was leading him on.

"What's the matter?" He frowned, looked back at the painting. "Don't you like it?"

"Matt." She laid a hand on his arm. "I'm the artist. That's my painting, and oddly enough, every word you said was true. That's exactly how I felt when I saw that scene."

He stepped back, his eyes narrowing a fraction. "You're the artist?" His lips started to curl in a delighted smile and he gestured from her to the painting and back again. "This is your work?" He glanced down at the catalogue and she could see his mind working. "A. Stewart. Ashley Stewart." He looked up again. "I didn't know your last name."

"I'm sorry, Matt. I didn't—"

He waved away her protestations. "No, don't be sorry. I'm not. Not at all." He looked back at the painting. "You're a very talented lady, but then I guess you know that."

"Thank you," she murmured, wishing she could learn to be more comfortable when people paid her a compliment.

"And to think that I almost didn't come tonight." Matt seemed to be looking at her with new eyes. "When I saw you yesterday, I thought I'd be back on the island by now, but then the invitation came—it was delayed in the mail—and when I saw the list of artists I changed my plans. I never miss a chance to see your work."

"Ah, there you are!" Gabrielle swept into the room. "I see you two have met at long last."

Matt and Ashley looked at each other and laughed, breaking any lingering tension.

"We know each other from Madrona Island," he volunteered. "As a matter of fact, we met on the ferry the day Ashley moved there." He returned his hand to her waist. The simple touch sent her senses reeling and she wanted to lean into him, to feel his arms around her.

"And I saw him again the very next day. Matt's daughter, Caitlin, sells produce at the Saturday morning market." She glanced at him with a smile. "She's quite the little entrepreneur."

"Of course she is." Gabrielle shrugged, but didn't give Ashley a chance to ask what she meant by that remark. "Can you come and meet some people, *chérie*? They're just leaving but they bought one of your pictures tonight." She turned to Matt. "You don't mind, I hope."

"Not at all, as long as she comes back to me." He grinned and her heart did a little somersault in her chest. "I haven't had a chance to ask her to dinner yet."

Gabrielle hustled Ashley up the stairs. "Their names are Amanda and Donald MacDonald."

"You're kidding, right?" Ashley forced down a giggle.

"No. That's why I came to get you. So I could warn you. Anyway, they bought the one you did of Cathedral Grove."

"I like that one."

"You like all of them." The gallery owner gave her a

gentle nudge. "When these customers have gone I want to hear all about Matthew Ryan."

The MacDonalds expressed their love for the painting and left the gallery, pleased to have met the artist. The display areas were still crowded, so Gabrielle drew Ashley into a corner of the kitchen. She fumbled in a drawer for her cigarette case, put one between her lips, and lit it, inhaling with satisfaction.

"So. I can't believe you know Matthew Ryan." Smoke came out of her nose and for a giddy moment Ashley thought she looked like a tiny dragon with a French accent. She looked at Ashley with dawning comprehension. "You don't know who he is, do you?"

"Should I?" What was Gabby getting at? "I know that he's a very charming man who welcomed me by taking me to lunch and buying me a hummingbird feeder. He has a delightful daughter and, well, that's all I know about him. Oh wait. I also know that he has an excellent tailor." She paused. "You say Ryan is his last name? Okay, that makes one more thing I know about him, but it doesn't make any difference. He's still the same man." She glanced toward the door, ensuring that she wouldn't be overheard. "He's rather handsome, wouldn't you say?"

"Mon Dieu." Gabrielle searched around for an ashtray then stubbed out her cigarette in the sink. "Ask any single woman and she'll tell you that Matthew Ryan is one of the most eligible bachelors in Vancouver."

"Matt?" Ashley darted a look toward the main gallery. "But why don't I know this?"

"But, *chérie*." Gabrielle's eyes softened. "You have been in another world for the last few years. Before that you were immersed in your painting, although come to think of it, it's only since his company went public a couple of years ago that he became notorious."

Ashley's heart sank. "You mean he's a womanizer?"

"Pas du tout." Gabrielle brushed Ashley's concerns aside. "Not at all. I meant that his name has started to appear in the papers and there have been a few appearances on television. He's the CEO of Angulus Technologies."

Ashley shook her head. "Angulus Technologies?"

The Frenchwoman looked heavenward in frustration. "Yes. I was reading about him and his company just last week. Angulus is mainly a software development company, and it's quoted as being the most successful start-up in the area." She held out her left hand, ticking off a point on each finger. "Employs two thousand people. Annual sales of almost seventy million dollars. Vancouver's most eligible bachelor. Boy genius turned entrepreneur."

"He lied to me." The smile on Ashley's face belied the harsh words. "He told me he's a computer geek."

"A computer geek who happens to own one of the most successful companies in Canada." Gabrielle leaned back against the counter, watching Ashley's reaction. "He's been a customer for a few years now and it's always been a pleasure to deal with him. Right now, I think he's waiting for you."

"Oh my goodness, yes." Ashley took a quick glance at her reflection in a small mirror then turned to her friend. "Do I look all right?"

Gabrielle smiled. "You look lovely, my dear." They wandered back into the gallery. "Enjoy yourself tonight."

Matt had made his way out to one of the smaller viewing rooms. He spotted her immediately and with a few quick strides he was across the room, his eyes never leaving her face.

"Did I tell you how wonderful you look tonight?" He picked up her hand and brushed his lips against it. "I hope you're free for dinner." He leaned closer and his scent invaded her senses. "Do you have to stick around very long? I took a chance that you'd be free for dinner and made a reservation, but I think they'll accommodate us whenever we arrive."

"I can leave any time." Ashley realized that she hadn't eaten any lunch. "Actually, I'm fairly hungry. I've been on the go all day long."

She joined Matt under the canopy after a quick good-bye to Gabrielle.

"I've called for the car. Ah, here it is now." A car pulled up and the valet jumped out. Matt waved him off and opened her door with a small flourish. Seeing him here—going out to dinner with him—was she dreaming?

Matt slid behind the wheel. "I can't believe you're actually here." His words echoed her thoughts. A boyish grin lit up his face. "If you only knew how many times I wanted to call you."

"Why didn't you?" she inquired tentatively.

"Because I wanted to let you settle in." She nodded and he continued. "Moving to the island must have been a difficult decision. I know if it had been me, I would have needed some time to adjust."

This man was dangerous. Even after years of marriage, Doug had never been as sympathetic to her moods as Matt seemed to be. And she barely knew him.

He was too perceptive, too considerate, too understanding. And far too appealing.

And yet, she could talk to him. Was that so bad? She settled back and decided to follow her instincts. "You were probably right. This may sound kooky, but while I was sleeping, reading, and just sitting out on the deck I began to feel the rhythms of the island. The movement of the tides, the flow of traffic to and from the ferries, even the way the residents make time to stop and say hello. They're all a part of living there that I've never experienced before."

He was listening intently, nodding as she spoke. "I know what you mean. Those are some of the things that keep me there. That, plus Caitlin is very happy on the island."

"Speaking of Caitlin, what about the market tomorrow? Who will take her?"

"Hopefully me. Betty and Archie are helping her load up the truck tonight. If I don't get home in time, Archie will drive her to the market and I'll catch up with her later."

Ashley scoured her memory for the ferry schedule. "But the first ferry won't get you home until midmorning."

"True, but I'm flying home in the morning, so I should make it on time." He took her hand. "Caity really enjoyed her visit with you this week. Thank you for being so patient with her."

"Not at all." Her entire body was suffused with heat from his touch. She continued in what she hoped was a normal tone. "As a matter of fact, it was her visit that inspired me to do the sketch I told you about. It's going to be my next project."

He reached across and gave her hand a quick squeeze. "I'm glad."

He turned into a broad driveway lit by elegant lamp standards. Lights reflected off the water and a discreet sign told her that they'd arrived at the finest seafood restaurant in Vancouver. Jessica had recently complained that they were booked two months in advance.

"Good to see you again, Mr. Ryan." The maître d' greeted Matt warmly. "I have your table ready, if you would care to follow me."

"Thank you for making room for us tonight." Matt guided her through the crowded room, his hand at her back. Several diners looked up as they passed, then did a double take. A murmur of recognition swept through the room and Ashley was relieved when they were settled at their table.

"I know I'm repeating myself but I'm blown away by the fact that you're here." Matt leaned back in his chair, looking hugely satisfied with himself. "My original plan was to go back to the office and work for a few hours tonight, but this is so much better." The waiter arrived with menus and asked if he could bring them something to drink.

"Perrier please." Ashley smiled up at him. "With some lemon."

Matt gave her an odd look. "Same for me." He handed back the wine menu and the waiter left.

"I hope you didn't order a nonalcoholic drink just because of me."

"Not at all." Something flickered behind his eyes. "For a while after Emily died, I was having trouble sleeping and I started to drink. At first it was a glass of brandy before bed, but before long I'd find myself reaching for a drink as soon as Caity was asleep." He gave his head a quick shake. "Fortunately, nothing bad ever happened because of it, but I decided that it could get out of hand very easily if I didn't stop. So I stopped."

"Not drinking isn't the only thing we have in common."

"Really?" His smile deepened the crinkles at the edge of his eyes.

"Really. You didn't know I was A. Stewart and I didn't know you were Mr. Angulus Technologies."

"Ah, yes." He nodded, acknowledging her point. "I have one of your paintings already, but I suppose Gabrielle told you that." She nodded and he continued. "Anyway, I must have looked at that signature a hundred times or more, but for some incomprehensible reason I always assumed that A. Stewart was a man."

"Sorry to disappoint you, although Ashley can be a man's name as well. *Gone with the Wind* and all that."

"Not my favorite movie, but you have a point." The waiter placed their drinks on the table. "Even when I saw the easel and paints at your home I didn't connect it, but of course I wouldn't, not knowing your last name."

"I wasn't trying to deceive you by not saying anything." She took a sip of her drink. "It's just that I don't tell most people about being a painter."

"Why not? You're amazing."

"Back at you. Why don't you tell people you're . . . how did Gabrielle put it? . . . 'one of the most successful start-ups in Canadian history.' Or something like that."

"That damned article." He picked up the menu, then set it back down. "I hate publicity."

She grinned at him. "Too late now."

Their eyes met for one long, intense moment. Then he picked up the menu again. "Everything is good here and you said you're hungry."

Chapter Seven

"My goodness." Ashley looked at the pile of scampi shells. "Did we eat all that?" She hadn't known that a restaurant meal could be so much fun. Matt had challenged her to try several dishes she'd never eaten before, and they'd ended the meal by ordering scampi.

"Sure did." He sat back with a satisfied sigh. "It's a pleasure to share a meal with someone who likes to eat."

"Me too." She dipped her fingers in the water bath. "But I'm not sure if I have any room for that chocolate mousse, and they're making it just for us." The plates were whisked away and their waiter appeared.

"Ah, Roger. Excellent as usual." Ashley liked the way he treated the restaurant staff. "Please tell the chef how much we enjoyed it."

"I will, sir. Do you still want coffee?"

Matt looked at Ashley and she nodded. "Coffee would be great."

It was just as well she didn't drink; his company was intoxicating enough. During dinner their conversation had covered a range of topics and she'd found herself leaning forward, captivated by his astute observations mixed with wry humor. He excused himself for a moment and she sat back with a sigh, her gaze drifting toward the darkened harbor. Across the water, the lights of downtown Vancouver, although familiar, suddenly seemed a part of her past. She'd grown up in Kerrisdale, on the far side of English Bay, and had spent most of her teenaged summers on the broad beaches. Learning to sail on the waters of English Bay had been a highlight of those carefree years and there were still times when she could hear the snap of the sails as they filled with air, and the rush of water against the hull.

"You look pensive." Matt was sliding into his chair.

"I was thinking about sailing." She gestured toward the water. "When I was a kid we had a small sailboat and we practically lived on English Bay in the summer. It was an ideal way to grow up."

"That's something else we have in common then." He thanked the server for the coffee and dessert, then continued. "I have a sailboat on the island."

"Do you keep it at the marina?"

"No, it's at my home. I had the good fortune to be able to buy several adjoining pieces of property encircling a small bay on the south end of the island." He gave a small, almost self-conscious shrug. "I guess you could say I like my privacy."

"It sounds wonderful."

"We think so." He cocked his head to one side, as though hearing a voice. "Did you drive over?"

"No, I came as a foot passenger."

"Good, because if you'd like to fly back with me in the morning, you're welcome. That is, if you're not seeing Jessica." He looked at her hopefully.

"Actually, Jessica is out of town this weekend." Ashley considered the offer. "What time do you leave?"

"That's the thing. You'd have to be at my Richmond office before seven in the morning." He paused to give her time to consider. "I could send a car for you."

Ashley didn't need any further encouragement. "That would be great. I have someone looking in on Honey, but even so, I've been worried about her."

"Good—that's settled."

The car was waiting as they left the restaurant and they were back at the hotel in what seemed like moments. Now that the evening was ending, Ashley wished that it could go on forever.

"I'll walk you to your room," he said, helping her from the car at the porte cochere. Ashley wondered if he could hear her heart pounding as they ascended silently in the elevator and walked to her door.

"I'll send the car to pick you up at six in the morning. Is that all right?"

She nodded, afraid to speak.

"Thank you for a wonderful evening. I enjoyed every

minute of it." He reached out and brushed aside a lock of hair that had escaped from the side of her head. The touch was gentle and she leaned her head into his hand, closing her eyes. When she opened them, a faint smile curved his lips and he lowered his head slowly, silently asking permission. She raised her lips to his, and his arms encircled her, pulling her against his broad chest. His kiss was exquisitely gentle, tentative even, and his tongue slowly teased her lips open. She leaned into him, savoring the almost-forgotten sensations. She pulled away slowly, fighting to regain her composure.

"Wow," she said breathlessly.

"You can say that again," he murmured, a crooked grin on his face. He leaned forward and kissed her on the forehead. "We'd better say good night if we're going to get any sleep."

"Right." She fumbled in her small clutch bag for the room card and managed to get it into the slot. "See you in the morning, then."

"I'll be waiting for you." He strode down the hallway, long-legged and oh so appealing.

Ashley leaned against the closed door, willing her heart to return to normal. His kiss had awakened sensations in her that had been dormant for a long time. She'd thought she liked it that way but now, with Matt Ryan in her life, she might have to rethink that.

Ashley was waiting in the lobby when the car arrived the next morning. The traffic was sparse at this hour on a Saturday morning and they pulled up in front of the Angulus building with plenty of time to spare.

"Mr. Ryan's office is on the top floor," the driver informed her. "He asked me to send you right up. I'll deliver your bag directly to the roof."

"The roof?" Ashley glanced up then motioned to Sea Island. "Aren't we going to the airport?" In the distance, aircraft could be seen landing and taking off.

"No. Mr. Ryan has his own helicopter."

This would take some getting used to. Ashley stepped into the elevator and exited into a tastefully appointed executive suite. Matt appeared down a long hallway, looking delicious in jeans and a denim shirt.

"I was up early this morning and thought I'd get in an hour of work." He stopped before her. "How did you sleep?"

"Surprisingly well." She glanced around. "Do you sleep here?"

"Sometimes, although I try to be home for Caity most nights. I have a small suite. Here, come and see my office. I know where you work. Now you can see where I toil away." He led the way to a large corner office. Ashley doubted that he spent much time gazing out the windows that overlooked the Fraser River delta, but it was a magnificent view. Her eyes swept the room, coming to rest on the wall above an informal seating area. Aware that he was watching her, she went closer. He had chosen a painting she'd done around four years ago, when she'd traveled to Barkerville, a former gold rush town in the Cariboo area of British Columbia.

"You like detail, I see," she said, gesturing to the painting. She'd been fascinated by the appearance of one of the buildings that had yet to be restored. It had been during the early summer and the contrast between the delicate fuchsia spikes of fireweed in the foreground and the weathered siding had called to her. She still remembered how small things about the building had tugged at her heart. Rust stains called attention to a horseshoe over the front door and faded curtains, now torn to shreds, showed that the building had been inhabited by people with hopes and dreams, people who had tried to carve out a place for themselves in what had been a wilderness area.

She turned to find him gazing at the painting.

"Emily and I went to Barkerville on our honeymoon. When I saw this painting I thought I recognized the scene, and when Gabrielle confirmed where it had been done I had to have it." He gave her a steady look. "At first I thought I'd made a mistake, because every time I looked at it I was reminded of Emily, but now it reminds me of happy times." He grinned. "Plus, I like it."

"I'm glad." Ashley didn't know what else to say.

He cocked his head, alert to a faint noise from outside. "I think our ride is here. Are you ready?"

He led her down a corridor and out onto the roof where a helicopter sat, rotors slowing. Taking her hand he led her out to the craft and settled her in the backseat with a set of headphones before climbing in beside the pilot. Suddenly the roof of the building was falling away below them and they were turning in a slow arc, heading out to the water. Breaking through the clouds, the morning sun cast a molten sheen on the dark water below.

"Are you all right back there?" Matt's voice came through the headset.

"Yes, I'm fine." Ashley craned her neck. "Look, you

can see Mount Baker." The magnificent mountain in Washington State glowed above the clouds in the morning sunlight.

Matt gave a running commentary as they flew over the Gulf of Georgia, naming the various islands. In no time at all, he was pointing out Madrona Island and Ashley looked down on the beautiful island that she'd quickly come to think of as home.

The helicopter rounded a headland and a small bay opened up below them, the water dark green and almost calm.

"That's our place down there," he informed her. "You can see the helipad."

It took only one glance for Ashley to see that Matt's home was magnificent. The sprawling complex appeared to grow out of the rock, spilling down the hillside as it followed the contours of the land. The colors blended into the surroundings and she could see that the structure had been built to accommodate several trees clinging to the rocky shoreline. Arbutus and Garry Oak trees dotted the sunny slope on either side of the house, and tall cedars provided a majestic backdrop. A sailboat sat quietly at anchor, her tall mast casting a long shadow in the morning sun.

The helicopter settled down slowly, affording Ashley time to observe Caitlin's garden, enclosed on four sides by a high wire fence. Matt opened her door and helped her out as Caitlin came running toward them.

"Daddy!" Caitlin leaped into his arms and wrapped her legs around his waist. "I missed you." She turned to Ashley, squirming to be let down. "Hi, Ashley." She looked from Ashley to her father. "Did Ashley go to the gallery with you, Daddy?"

Matt squatted down, eye to eye with his daughter. "Do you remember the painting in my office? The one of the old building?" Caitlin nodded soberly. "Well, Ashley is the artist who painted it. I found that out last night."

Caitlin's eyes widened. "Are you a real painter?"

Ashley laughed. "I think so. I've been practicing a long time."

The child tugged at her father's hand. "I'm all ready for the market. Archie put my stuff in the truck already. Are you coming?"

"Of course I'm coming." He laid a hand on her head and Ashley was touched by the display of affection. "I'm going to set up your table and unload your stuff, then drive Ashley home while you're arranging your produce."

Caitlin chattered nonstop on the way to the market, relating her adventures of the previous night's sleep-over. Ashley sat quietly in the back, admiring the way Matt gave the child his full attention.

They worked together, setting up Caitlin's table and tent, and unloading the boxes of produce. The youngster was already arranging her vegetables as Matt and Ashley climbed into the truck, but she stopped and ran to the passenger side of the vehicle.

"Can I come and see you again this week?" Her eyes communicated her eagerness.

"Yes, of course. Do you still have my phone number?" The child nodded. "Then phone me anytime and I'll watch for you." The child smiled, and to her surprise

Ashley found that she was already looking forward to another visit.

They drove home with the windows open and Ashley breathed deeply, savoring the woodsy smell of the island. Sunlight flickered through the trees and she gave a loud sigh of contentment.

"That was a big one." Matt glanced at her sideways. "Is everything all right?"

"More than all right. I'm really starting to love it here." He slowed down as they approached her turnoff. "On the way over here I realized how much."

Matt nodded. "I'm glad you feel that way." He turned into her driveway and leaped out to help her down. "What about this afternoon? Will you be coming to the marina for lunch?"

Ashley looked into his eyes and her gaze slid to his mouth. More than anything, she wanted to spend time with this man, but her instincts warned her to slow down. Besides, he'd been away from home overnight, away from his daughter.

"I think maybe I should leave you and Caitlin alone for today." Disappointment flashed in his eyes, but she also sensed that he respected her decision. "I hope you understand."

He reached out for her and drew her closer. "You are a very special lady, Ashley Stewart. I hate to admit it, but I think you're right." He tipped up her chin. "I'd like to see you again though. Is that okay with you?"

"I'd like that," she murmured.

He cupped her head with both hands and brushed his lips against hers, a sweet kiss filled with promise. "I'll be seeing you soon," he whispered, then turned and got into the vehicle.

Ashley opened the sliding glass doors leading to the deck and inhaled the now-familiar ocean air. A flash of movement caught her eye and she looked up in time to see the feisty little hummingbird rocketing straight up in the air. He seemed to pause, then swooped down again near the edge of the deck, making a raspy *zzzt* sound. She watched as he flew the pattern over and over again, always with the buzzing sound at the bottom of the parabola. A few moments later she noticed a second hummingbird on the feeder. Slightly drabber, with no brilliance under the throat, the new bird must be a female, Ashley realized, and she felt a sudden kinship with the tiny creature, caught up in the eternal rituals of male-female courtship.

Chiding herself for indulging in fanciful daydreams, she wandered back into the house and slid onto the stool in the studio. She'd placed a blank canvas on the easel as inspiration, but it was Matt's face that swam before her eyes. Unconsciously she raised a hand to her lips, recalling the way he'd held her last night, the way his lips had ignited sparks of desire in the ashes of her soul. No, she told herself, she hadn't imagined it. Matt Ryan was the real deal.

Matt lounged in a folding canvas chair, watching as Caitlin rearranged the produce on her table, spreading out the few remaining items.

"Looks like you're going to sell out today."

She walked over to stand beside him and leaned her arm on his shoulder. "Yes, it's been a good day."

Matt held back a smile. His little entrepreneur could be so serious about her produce stand. Abruptly, she became a little girl again. "Is Ashley going to meet us at the marina today?" she inquired.

Matt gave her a startled look. He had just been thinking about Ashley, wishing that she had accepted his invitation.

"Not today, sweetie." He decided to bend the truth a little, knowing that Caitlin would not understand Ashley's reasoning. "She had some work to do at home."

Caitlin bit her bottom lip. "That's too bad. I like her a lot." She peered into her father's eyes. "Do you like her, Daddy?"

He held her around the waist, nodding thoughtfully. "I'm still getting to know her but yes, I do like her."

The clear green eyes looked at him steadily. "I'm still getting to know her too, but I think she's very nice. And I think she likes you too."

Matt looked at his daughter in amazement and was grateful when another customer came to the table. Caitlin was becoming far too perceptive.

Overcome by the urge to paint, Ashley gathered up her outdoor painting kit, her bag, and a fresh canvas. Honey wiggled with delight and led the way down to the beach, where Ashley set her canvas on a small easel designed for just that purpose.

The rocky beach took shape quickly under her skilled brush strokes, and she smiled at the image she was creating; it was as if she'd never been away from painting. Paige had often accompanied her on painting excursions and she missed her daughter, who would often read quietly by her side. She raised her eyes to the sky and in that moment she knew that Paige would always be with her. It was a comforting thought, and she returned her concentration to the painting, filling in the background details. She looked forward to Caitlin's next visit, when she could more accurately capture the expression on the child's face as she peered into the tidal pool. A sudden thought stilled her brush. The painting would make an ideal gift for Matt to thank him for the helicopter ride.

The sun rose higher, and the glare from the water drove her back into the house. As she was climbing the stairs, her cell phone rang in her pocket.

"Hi there. It's Gloria. How is Honey?"

Ashley felt a momentary stab of guilt that she had not yet called to tell the other woman she'd returned. She walked up the last few steps and Honey flopped down on the deck. "She's fine, and thank you for looking in on her."

"It was no trouble at all. Listen, Ashley, I called to ask you if you'd like to join our Little Theater group. We're getting ready for our fall season and I'm calling around to touch base with everyone who's expressed an interest. Brenda said to give you a call."

"I'm not sure I'd be much help, but it sounds interesting."

"That's great. There aren't very many of us, so we can always use another pair of hands. And we have a lot of fun."

"Brenda said I might be of some help in set painting. Would there be someone there to show me what to do?"

"Oh sure. Fran is acting in the play this fall, but she has done lots of sets. She could show you the tricks of the trade, as it were."

"Okay, then put me down. When do you expect to start?" This was beginning to sound like fun.

"I'll call you soon and give you the date, okay?" Gloria sounded pleased.

Ashley smiled to herself. Becoming part of this small community appealed to her and she looked forward to getting to know some local residents. Turning on the CD player, she went back to work with a light heart, and was soon immersed in her painting.

The telephone broke into her concentration and she put down her brush with a frown. Two calls in one afternoon. A new record. "Hello," she answered gaily.

"Well aren't you the cheerful one." Jessica's familiar voice lightened her spirits even farther. "You sound like you won the lottery."

Ashley slipped off the stool and ran her fingers through her hair. "It's better than that. I'm having a good day," she replied, looking out the window to where clouds were building in the west. "And you're my second phone call this afternoon. How are you, anyway?"

"I'm great. How was the opening?"

"According to Gabby, it was a great success. I thought she was going to run out of little red dots."

"Excellent. So, are you sitting down?" Ashley knew that teasing tone. It was probably being accompanied by some severe eyebrow wiggling—Jessica's imitation of Groucho Marx.

"Okay. What now?" Ashley tried to sound disinterested, but that was difficult when her friend got started. Just in case, she wandered out to the deck and stretched out on the lounge.

"Well, my little recluse, you're not going to believe what I dug up on your friend Matthew."

"Jessica! You promised you wouldn't. And anyway I—"

"I can't help it, Ash, you know that. I'm a nosy journalist. So sue me."

Jessica's brash ways were tempered with genuine caring, and Ashley found it hard to be annoyed with her longtime friend. And to be truthful, she was curious about what Jessica had discovered.

"I know you want to hear what I found out."

Jessica's words echoed her own thoughts. "Okay, Sherlock, what's the scoop?"

"First of all, your tall, handsome admirer is an incredibly successful businessman. He owns Angulus Technologies. You know, the software company out in Richmond? Anyway, I didn't think you'd know much about them, so I dug up some information for you."

Ashley heard her friend shuffling some papers.

"Let's see. Oh yes, here it is. This one is a couple of years old. 'The eagerly anticipated IPO of Angulus Technologies took place this week. The share offering was oversubscribed by four hundred percent, and made the company's CEO, Matthew Ryan, an instant billionaire.

Angulus' knowledge and expertise in software applications, combined with their recent entry into security systems have made them the preferred supplier to government, banks, and big business worldwide.'" Jessica paused. "I probably should have recognized him when I met him at your place last week, but evidently he guards his privacy and doesn't give very many interviews, so I can be forgiven for not putting two and two together."

Ashley broke into the conversation. "Jess, I know about his business. He came to the opening last night." Her voice softened. "He was just standing there, looking at one of the paintings. At first I thought I was imagining it but it was him all right."

"You mean the elusive Matthew Ryan is an art lover?" Ashley could almost hear her friend digesting this information. "Well, why not? He can surely afford to buy anything he likes. So tell me, how did you find out about his business?"

"Gabby told me, and then Matt filled me in a bit more over dinner."

"So it's Matt now, is it?" Jessica's voice lowered. "Do tell."

Ashley laughed. "Don't get all carried away. We had a lovely dinner, and we flew back together this morning." Realizing how that sounded, she added quickly, "He sent someone to pick me up at the hotel."

"Huh. This guy may be something of an enigma, but what little is written about him is absolutely glowing."

"Really?" Ashley had to ask. "Like what?"

"You see? You really do want to know. I knew it! Just a sec." There was more paper shuffling, and then Jessica came back on the line. "They make him sound like a paragon of virtue, if you'll pardon an overused expression. Listen to what I dug up from an interview that took place a few years ago. 'Matthew Ryan unerringly guided Angulus Technologies through the vagaries of the recent tech meltdown with a combination of incredible foresight and rigid business ethics. He is not a man to be crossed in the "take-no-prisoners" world in which he operates, but his honesty and integrity have made him one of the most respected CEOs in his field.' "

Ashley sat back, a smile on her face. "Somehow that doesn't surprise me, Jess. There's something about him . . ."

"So when are you going to see him again?"

"I don't know, but I'm pretty sure I'll hear from him." It was too soon to tell her friend that she was falling for the irresistible Matt Ryan. Besides, some secrets were better savored alone.

Matt sat quietly on the spacious deck of his home, coffee cup in hand. These sun-splashed summer mornings were special to him, and he cherished the rare moments alone. Squinting against the sun's glare, he studied the sleek lines of his sailboat. It had been too long since he'd felt the thrill of being out on the water. Between Caitlin and the demands of business there was very little time for his own pleasures, but he wouldn't change a thing. He took a swallow of coffee and eyed the boat thoughtfully. Loving and caring for his daughter didn't mean he had to deny his own yearnings. Yearnings that had started several weeks ago . . .

Meeting Ashley on the ferry that first day had been a small miracle. He rarely took the ferry, preferring the speed and convenience of the helicopter. Any number of people could have arranged for a bicycle for Caity's birthday, but she had been so excited when he'd discussed it with her, and so specific as to which one she wanted. Every executive worth his pay knew that some things just had to be done in person, and buying his daughter's birthday present had been one of those things. It chilled him to think that if he hadn't been on the ferry he might never have met Ashley.

He'd been curious about her from the moment he spotted her on the deck, clutching the railing as though in pain. She'd been holding back tears, he was sure of it, and he almost hadn't approached her. But something about her had drawn him, and he'd waited while she composed herself. When she'd raised her eyes, looking at him with that open, honest gaze, it was as if someone had given his heart a gentle squeeze. And now she crept into his thoughts at the most surprising moments, and he found himself wanting to be with her, to see her face light up as she spoke.

"Would you care for some more coffee, Matthew?" The housekeeper bustled out onto the deck, coffeepot in hand. It had been a real victory when he'd convinced the housekeeper and her husband to call him by his first name.

"I'd love some, Betty." He held up his cup. "I thought you and Archie were taking the day off."

"We are, we are. We're on our way out now and I just wondered if you needed anything."

"No thanks. You two have a good day."

His thoughts drifted back to Ashley. She was a flesh-and-blood woman—her kiss had convinced him of that—but in many ways she was like a frightened woodland creature. Was it any wonder, he mused, after knowing that her marriage was disintegrating, and then losing her daughter? It had taken all his self-restraint not to call her while she settled in, but he'd known instinctively that she needed time, and if there was one thing he'd learned from his business, it was patience.

Caitlin wandered out of the house in her pajamas, rubbing the sleep out of her eyes.

"What are you going to do today, pumpkin?" he asked as she came to stand beside his chair, blinking in the sunlight.

"I don't know, Daddy. Kimberly and I were thinking about going for a bike ride. I checked my garden yesterday afternoon and there aren't any weeds to be pulled." Caitlin was relentless in her pursuit of weeds. "What are you going to do?"

"I was thinking about inviting Ashley over for dinner." He was pleased to see his daughter's face break into a smile. "What do you think about that?"

"Do we get to cook our own dinner?" The child loved to help in the kitchen, and the weekends were their special time to cook together.

"Yes, but let's keep it informal. Steak or chicken on the grill, some baked potatoes, and a nice fresh salad."

"And some ice cream for dessert," announced Caitlin. "Can we call her now?"

Matthew glanced at his watch. "It's a bit early. Let's give her another hour, and then I'll call."

Ashley was padding around in her bare feet when the phone rang. She'd stayed up late the night before watching an old Cary Grant movie, and she was barely awake.

"I hope I didn't wake you."

His voice was low and intimate, making her heart skitter around in her chest. "If you'd called ten minutes ago I would have said yes. How are you this beautiful morning?" It was even more beautiful now that he'd called.

"Caity and I were wondering if you'd like to come over and keep us company for dinner tonight. It'll be just the three of us."

"That's the best offer I've had all day." He chuckled, and she pictured the laugh lines around his eyes. "What time should I show up?"

"Come on by anytime this afternoon and I can give you the ten-cent tour of the place."

"Sounds great. See you later." Ashley disconnected and smiled to herself. This afternoon couldn't come soon enough.

Matthew hummed as he checked the charcoal in the barbecue. He had poured an entire bottle of marinade over some chicken pieces earlier, and three perfectly marbled rib-eye steaks sat on a plate covered with clear wrap. Caitlin had insisted on adding corn to the menu, and the cobs sat off to the side, slathered with butter and foil-wrapped. There was enough food for a thrashing, but he didn't care. Today was special.

He wandered out to Caitlin's garden and picked some mesclun, some fresh radishes, and a bunch of green onions. The addition of some store-bought cherry tomatoes would make a simple salad.

The sound of tires crunching on gravel caught his attention and he looked up just as Ashley's van appeared. Through the open window her hair looked like spun gold as she drove through patches of sunlight and his heart skipped a beat at the sight of her. Closer to the house, the trees had been cleared, making way for a workshop, parking area, and the caretaker's cottage. The clearing also allowed enough light for Caitlin's garden to thrive.

Ashley parked beside the Land Rover and got out slowly, taking in her surroundings. Spotting him, she waved and walked slowly toward him. Dressed simply in a scoop-neck top and a long wraparound skirt, she picked her way along the path leading to the garden.

"Hello again." She stopped outside the garden fence with the sun at her back, her gaze steady on his face, as though seeing him for the first time.

Matt was suddenly clumsy, unsure of himself. He gathered up the radishes and placed them in Betty's gardening basket, then pushed open the gate of the tall fence. "Come on in and see Caitlin's garden. She's out with her friend right now on her bike."

Ashley smiled at the sight of the neat rows and the

staked tomatoes. She wouldn't have expected any less of Caitlin. "She's quite the gardener, isn't she?"

Matt permitted himself a proud grin. "Yes, she is, although I suppose it could be genetic."

She gave him a curious look. "You come from a farming background?"

"You could call it that. I grew up in the Okanagan, and for several generations back we were in the fruit business. Back then, we grew cherries and apples, but the farm switched over to grapes five or six years ago."

"And did you help out when you were younger?" Her eyes never left his face.

"You'd better believe it. We were luckier than some of the other kids, though. Our cherries came off fairly early in the summer and then we were free to work elsewhere picking soft fruit until the apples were ready in the fall." He grinned at the memory. "We didn't get paid for working at home, but we could earn money picking for other orchards. Nowadays the kids can't be bothered. Most of the pickers are from Quebec. Recently there have even been some from Mexico." He shook his head. "I never thought I'd see the day when local kids thought they were too good to pick fruit."

Ashley glanced back at the garden. "Is that why you encourage Caitlin to grow things and sell them at the market?"

He nodded. "I suppose that's part of it, although it wasn't my idea to begin with. She started off being interested in seed germination. You probably remember putting the bean seed in a glass with a wet piece of absorbent paper and watching it germinate. Her class at school did that and her interest just sort of grew from there, no pun intended." He picked up the basket. "At first when she said she wanted to try to sell her produce I was concerned that the local farmers would resent her, but I didn't give them enough credit. The ones who sell their produce at the market aren't trying to make a living from it; they welcomed her like one of them." He shook his head. "You should hear them discussing varieties of tomatoes."

Ashley walked out of the gate and waited while he closed up. "Next thing you know, she'll be wanting a greenhouse."

"She already does. I'm going to buy her a small one and I think I'll let her pay for part of it. I don't ever want her to end up like those kids who expect handouts from their parents."

She looked up at him for a long, intense moment. "You're a good father, Matthew Ryan." A cloud seemed to pass over her eyes and he wondered if she was remembering her daughter. Then she smiled, and it was like the sun coming out. "What's next on the tour?"

Matt's home was everything she thought it would be. Designed around the spectacular ocean view, each room featured large windows, taking the open design one step further. Built on several layers, the home flowed down the hillside, leading the eye toward the sheltered bay and the ocean beyond. Ashley paused in the great room, taking it all in. She didn't know quite what she'd expected . . . perhaps a decorator-designed home without a heart. She should have known better; Matt's home was

informal and welcoming. He led her up three wide steps
to the kitchen and placed the basket containing the salad
makings on the counter. On the other side of the kitchen,
an informal dining room led to a spacious sunroom,
which appeared to be the most popular room in the
house. A telescope in one corner confirmed this fact, and
beyond the sunroom the outdoor deck followed the contours of the house, creating several separate areas dotted
with comfortable furniture.

He swept his arm toward the deck. "Would you like
to sit outside? Something to drink perhaps? I have Perrier and Pellegrino."

"I like both. You choose." She wandered back into
the kitchen as he filled two glasses. "You have a lovely
home. It has good vibes."

He looked around, a smile on his face. "It does,
doesn't it? Caity and I enjoy it." He touched her shoulder gently as he led her outside.

Sitting contentedly in a lounge chair she gazed out at
the water. The sailboat rode silently at anchor, its single
mast pointing toward the sky. "How long is the boat?"
she asked, sizing it up. "About thirty feet?"

"You have a good eye. It's a thirty-two-footer."

"I'm no expert, but it has lovely lines." Ashley tilted
her head and admired the classic shape.

"It's designed by Bill Garden. They don't come any
better, in my opinion." His eyes swept over the boat and
she saw a flash of nostalgia.

"Have you always sailed?"

He tore his gaze away from the boat and sat down beside her. "Our family lived close to a lake, so we all

sailed from an early age, but it wasn't the same as sailing on the ocean. When I came to Vancouver and earned some money it was one of the first things I bought. I've never regretted it." He smiled into the distance.

"And the telescope?" She glanced over her shoulder. "Are you whale watching?"

"Yes. The orcas often go right by here. Have you seen any yet by your place?"

"No, unfortunately. I've kept my eyes open, but not yet."

"Too bad—they're magnificent creatures. If I had more time I'd be actively involved in trying to protect their environment, but there are only so many hours in the day and Caity is my first priority." He gave a small shrug. "But I help out when I can."

"Which is a lot more than some people." Ashley swung her feet onto the deck and stood up. "Shall we make that salad now? I'd like to feel I'm doing something."

They chatted easily in the spacious kitchen, and had just finished tidying up when Caitlin came bouncing through the front door.

"Hi, Ashley. Hi, Daddy. Kimberly and I found the neatest tidal pool over on East Side road. I think I really will be a marine biologist when I grow up."

"And I know you'd be a great one." Matt's love for his daughter shone from his eyes. "But I hope you'll be careful on those rocks. The seaweed can make them slippery." He turned to Ashley. "We saw a documentary last night about a marine biologist and Caity thought that would be a pretty good way to earn a living."

"I could be outside all the time, not stuck in an office

like Daddy," she said, climbing up on a stool. "Did you see my garden, Ashley?"

"Yes, I did, and it's wonderful. I'm amazed that you don't have any weeds."

"Betty says I'm going to kill the plants with kindness. I don't think that's possible, do you?"

"Well, I hope not, because it looks fantastic to me." She noted a gold heart around the girl's neck and remembered the beads in her purse. "I just remembered, I brought you something from Vancouver."

The child's eyes brightened and followed Ashley's movements as she picked up her purse and dug into it. Matt stood back and watched the exchange with interest.

"Here you go. I hope you like them."

Caitlin opened the bag and spilled the shell chips out onto the counter.

"And I brought you all the findings to go with them. You know, wire and clasp and all that stuff." She handed her another bag. "You've done it before, haven't you?"

"Yes, but only with black cord." She examined everything carefully. "This is going to be so cool."

"Good. The saleslady gave me enough material to make two. You know, in case you and Kimberly want to have matching necklaces."

Caitlin threw both arms around Ashley's neck and kissed her on the cheek. "Thank you," she said, eyes shining. "I'm going to go and phone Kimberly right now." She ran off down the hall, then turned to run back. "Thanks again. These are so neat."

In all the excitement Ashley hadn't noticed Matt's retreat back to the sundeck. He stood at the railing, looking out at a passing trawler. He turned as she walked up beside him, his expression unreadable, then looked back out over the water, shaking his head.

"What's the matter?" She could see that he was troubled.

"I sometimes wonder if I'm doing things right when it comes to Caity. You've only met her a couple of times and you knew what she wanted."

She laid a hand on his arm. "It's only girl stuff. It's not that important."

"But what worries me is that maybe I'm missing some of the bigger things too."

"Like what?"

"That's just it, I don't know."

Ashley took a deep breath. "I'm no expert, but I can see that you give that girl lots of what she needs most in life. You give her love. What's more, you're teaching her to respect nature, to work for what she wants, and to be independent. Those things are beyond value. As far as I can tell, you're doing everything right."

"I like to think so. I didn't mean to sound like I was feeling sorry for myself. I just want to be a good father." He shot her a curious look. "Are your parents still alive?"

Ashley was startled at the question. "My mom died when I was quite young, but my father remarried a wonderful woman a few years ago. They live in a retirement community in Ontario and they love it." She paused. "Why do you ask?"

He gave her a lop-sided grin. "Talking about what Caity needs made me think about my mom. She and my sister are always trying to set me up whenever I visit them. They seem to think Caity needs a mother."

Ashley was surprised by the sudden wave of jealousy that washed over her at the thought of Matt with another woman. Somehow she had always pictured him as alone—a ridiculous assumption now that she thought about it.

She forced herself to smile. "They just want you to be happy. I don't think they mean it as criticism when they try to fix you up."

A breeze came up and toyed with her hair. He brushed it away from her face, and his hand lingered on her cheek. "Ashley Stewart, you are one sweet lady," he said, his voice deep and throaty. Leaning over, he kissed her on the cheek, lingering a moment. "Is that violets I smell?"

Ashley felt a blush rising up from her neck to her face. "Call me old-fashioned, but yes, it is. I love the delicate fragrance, even though it doesn't last very long. How did you know?"

"My grandmother loved the scent of violets. She was a tiny little thing and she worked right alongside my grandfather in the orchards. But when she got dressed up she smelled like that." He pulled back and looked her up and down. "Know what? You don't look anything like my grandmother!"

They laughed together and he put the steak and chicken on the barbecue as Caitlin came out onto the deck.

They ate at a picnic table on the deck and Ashley was astounded at Caitlin's appetite. The child ate everything on her plate, bright eyes darting back and forth between Ashley and Matt as they chatted casually about island life.

"Do you know how to play Clue?" Caitlin was helping to load the dishwasher.

"As a matter of fact, I do." Ashley watched as Caitlin added the dishwashing liquid. "Which character do you like?"

"Miss Scarlet, and Daddy likes Colonel Mustard. Who do you like?"

"I was always Professor Plum, although being a professor didn't help me to play any better."

"Would you like to play? I can get the board out and get it ready."

"Is she trying to talk you into playing Clue?" asked Matt, coming in from the deck. "I thought I heard something about Colonel Mustard."

Ashley smiled. "It's been a long time, but I'm willing to give it a go if you are."

Caitlin giggled as Matt scowled ferociously. "Okay, but I warn you, we play to win."

Matt called a halt after three games. "Time for you to go to bed, young lady." He rumpled Caitlin's hair. "Say good night to Ashley."

Caitlin gathered up the game pieces and came to stand beside Ashley. "I'll try to get to visit you before I go to camp."

Ashley had forgotten about their earlier conversation. "When do you leave?"

"I think it's Wednesday." She turned to Matt. "That's right, isn't it, Daddy?"

"Yes, sweetie. It's coming up pretty soon."

Caitlin threw her arms around Ashley's neck for the second time that day. "Good night, Ashley, and thanks again for the beads."

Ashley returned the hug. "You're welcome, Caity. Sleep well."

The child ran off and Ashley turned to Matt. "Thanks for a wonderful evening. I really enjoyed myself." She gathered up her purse. "I'm going to leave now and let you say good night to Caitlin."

He walked her slowly to the door. "It was fun, wasn't it?"

The outdoor lights had come on as dusk fell, but there was still a pale pink wash of color in the sky. He walked beside her toward the van.

"This doesn't feel right," he said with a wry smile. "I'm supposed to be saying good night to you at your place." He took a step closer. "Then I might get a good-night kiss."

Chapter Eight

His face was partly in shadows, but his eyes were luminous as he smiled down at her. "So let's make it right," she whispered, raising herself on tiptoes, kissing him lightly on the lips.

"Yes, let's do that." His hand brushed the side of her cheek, traced the line of her jaw and came to rest on the side of her neck. Shivering in anticipation, she raised her lips again and his mouth found hers. Both arms were around her now, his hands sliding down her back as he pulled her closer. His kiss was gentle and yet demanding, sweet and yet passionate. She opened her eyes and found him looking down at her. In the soft glow of the gathering twilight time seemed to stand still as they gazed into each other's eyes. This was where she wanted to be, enfolded in the safety of his arms. They stood that way for a few moments, hearts pounding.

Ashley pulled back slowly, hesitant to break the spell.

"Caitlin," she murmured, with a glance toward the house. "She's probably waiting."

He nodded and opened the door of the van, assisting her into the driver's seat. "Good night, Ashley," he murmured softly. "Thank you for coming."

Matt watched her pull away. She'd looked so lovely tonight; he'd been aching to kiss her from the moment she arrived, and it had been worth the wait. As he turned to go back into the house he thought he caught the scent of violets, and he smiled.

Ashley didn't remember driving home. Her skin still tingled from Matt's touch and she closed her eyes, losing herself in the memory of his lips on hers. Greeting Honey absently, she wandered into the studio, oblivious to the partly finished painting on the easel. Outside the last rays of light were slipping away and she slid herself onto the stool, deep in thought.

What was happening with Matt was too good to be true. The man was appealing on so many different levels she didn't know where to begin, but nobody could be that perfect—and everybody knew what that meant. It had grown darker in the last few moments and she looked at her reflection in the window. She'd always tried to be honest with herself, and she called upon that quality now. Unusual as it may be, it seemed that Matt Ryan had no faults, at least as far as she knew. He had been truthful and straightforward with her from the first moment they met. So what was bothering her? Was it that niggling feeling of guilt that she could actually laugh and enjoy an evening with Caitlin instead of Paige? She shook her head sadly. That type of self-recrimination was a waste of time. Paige was gone—a delightful and heartbreaking memory to be sure, but she was gone, and she wasn't coming back.

She went into the kitchen and made a cup of tea, her thoughts returning to Matt. Perhaps this new relationship was simply moving too quickly. She leaned on the counter while the water boiled, and she recalled the time she'd spent with him. Visions of his laughing eyes and long, elegant body competed with memories of his lips on hers. She groaned aloud. It was difficult to be analytical in the face of how he made her feel. *And yet* . . . a cautionary voice in the back of her mind whispered to her, making little pinpricks of apprehension march down her spine.

Mug of tea in hand, she found herself in front of the sliding glass windows, gazing out to where the running lights of a sailboat were visible just offshore. Being with Matt and Caitlin, she'd felt like part of a family, and it had been a seductive feeling. As an only child with no mother, she'd never experienced that special glow of belonging to a family group at play, and it was something she longed for. Tonight she'd had a taste of that elusive dream; it had been fun, but maybe it would be better not to become too attached to the idea. Even though it felt so right. . . .

The next morning Ashley pushed the previous night's doubts to the back of her mind. The sun was out again, and she intended to take advantage of the early morning light. Gathering up Honey and her sketching materials, she set out to tour the island. A winding road circled the perimeter, offering tantalizing glimpses of the ocean, then plunged back into the cool shadows of tall cedars. The tide was out this morning, and she noticed a small island just offshore, connected to the main island by a narrow causeway of rock. Tidal pools glinted in the shallows, and Ashley took a second look. This was probably the area where Caitlin and her friend had been playing yesterday. Driving on, she spotted the old farmhouse she'd noticed on her first day. The trees had almost finished blooming and pale petals drifted to the ground as she framed the scene in her mind. The workmen had finished with the house and the structure stood proudly in the sun at the end of a long driveway.

She set out her easel and folding chair, donned her straw hat, and was soon lost in the creative process. She had almost finished her preliminary sketch when the sharp beep of a car's horn startled her. She looked up as Brenda pulled off the road and stepped out.

"Hi there. I just stopped by to say hello." The Realtor smiled broadly. "I spoke to Gloria yesterday and she says you'll be helping out with set painting for our fall production."

Ashley tipped back her hat and looked up. "She assures me that someone will be able to show me the tricks of the trade." She hesitated. "I've never been much of a joiner. This will be a whole new experience for me."

"Well, we're glad to have your help. I think you'll find that everybody gets along well." Brenda raised her eyebrows. "And if there's anything in the wind that will affect our island lifestyle, it's sure to be thoroughly discussed."

Ashley was beginning to wonder what she was getting into. "I'm not sure what you mean. Is there something I should be aware of?"

The Realtor waved her hand as though clearing the air. "Sorry. I didn't mean to sound like we're a bunch of gossips or anything like that. It's just that anything affecting our coveted island way of life is often discussed in these small community groups before it becomes common knowledge. You'll be on the inside track for any earth-shattering developments." She laughed. "Not that anything earth-shattering happens around here."

"And with good reason. Take this old farmhouse, for example. On the mainland, this place would be torn down, but here it's been lovingly restored. This type of atmosphere can't be created overnight."

"True enough. Listen, I'd better get out of your way and let you continue on. Check out those clouds. You may get rained on soon."

Ashley stood up, stretched, and scanned the sky to the west. Brenda was right; it looked as though the idyllic summer weather was coming to an end. She worked quickly to finish the sketch and managed to pack up just in time to avoid the first raindrops. Running to the van, she loaded her supplies just as the skies opened up. "Sorry, Honey," she said, turning on the windshield wipers. "No walk on the beach for us today."

On the top floor of the Angulus Technologies building Matt walked his guest back to the reception area and shook hands. He had made it a policy never to shut himself away in his office, away from new ideas. As a result, his days were often spent in nonstop meetings with people from outside his own organization. Striding back into his office he noticed the sheets of rain sweeping across the delta. He picked up his telephone and dialed the now-familiar number.

Ashley's phone rang as she was dashing into the house. "Hello?" she gasped, struggling to balance her supplies.

"What are you doing? You sound like you're out of breath." Matt's familiar voice brought her to a standstill. She leaned back against the wall and pictured his face, which wasn't hard—she'd been thinking about him every spare moment since she'd woken up.

"I was out sketching and I just barely got my stuff in the car before it started to pour. It's coming down in buckets!" She giggled. "It's actually quite wonderful, now that I'm inside."

"I just noticed it raining here, and I was thinking about you over there with your first storm. Did you get very wet?" The tenderness in his voice made her heart beat faster.

"Just a little. All I could think of on the way home was a nice cup of hot tea."

"Well, make sure you dry off." He paused. "It's good to hear your voice, Ashley."

Swallowing hard, she tried to sound casual. "You too. Thanks for calling."

*   *   *

Matt stood in front of the window and gazed out into the rain. He pictured Ashley running from the rain and for one crazy moment he pictured himself toweling her hair dry, making her a cup of tea, breathing in her scent. He'd never heard her giggle before and his heart had lifted at the sound. They'd only known each other a few weeks, but last night's kiss had touched him deeply, and he couldn't wait to see her again. He snorted softly and looked around his office. Wouldn't his business associates be stunned to know that Matthew Ryan, tough competitor and board member of several major corporations, was mooning over a woman like a lovesick schoolboy!

He strode out to his secretary's office, catching her by surprise.

"Mr. Ryan, what can I do for you?"

"I'd like to take some flowers home tonight, Carole."

"Of course, Mr. Ryan. What type of arrangement?" She looked up, her pencil poised.

"What I'd like is a small bunch of violets." His eyes sparkled. "Do you think that would be possible?"

"Leave it with me, sir. Our florist can usually fill any request." She looked at her computer screen, which displayed his schedule. "Are you still leaving here at three o'clock?"

"Sure am. Thanks, Carole." He paused. "Could you please have the cafeteria send up a light lunch? I need to spend the next few hours studying that report from La Perouse, so please hold all my calls."

Matt served on the board of directors of La Perouse Explorations, one of the largest oil exploration companies in North America. It was no secret that the company would benefit if the Canadian government lifted the moratorium on oil and gas exploration on the West Coast. On his desk was the company's most recent report, detailing their intention to ramp up their effort to have the moratorium lifted. As always, he intended to go into the next meeting armed with all the facts at his disposal. Clearing his mind, he opened the report, and was soon applying his prodigious powers of concentration to the facts and statistics before him.

Ashley put on a CD of Andrea Bocelli and settled down with her mug of tea. She had no idea what the words meant, but the thrilling voice of the Italian tenor suited her mood. With rain pounding on the deck, Honey curled up at her feet and the romantic music playing in the background, her thoughts turned to Matt. His voice on the phone had been deep and intimate, and memories of last night came crowding back. She replayed the evening in her mind, images flickering across her consciousness like an old, stuttering movie. If only she could predict how that movie would end. . . .

Reeling herself back in, she sat up abruptly. "Enough daydreaming," she said aloud. "Time to get back to work." Picking up her mug of tea, she was soon humming to herself as the apple orchard started to come alive on the canvas. The afternoon slipped away and she didn't notice that the rain had stopped until a shaft of sunlight broke through the clouds, causing steam to rise from the rocky outcrop outside the window.

Startled by the doorbell, she glanced at her watch. Four o'clock already! The day had slid by without her realizing it. Preoccupied, she walked down the hall and threw open the door.

"Matt! I was just thinking about you." The words tumbled out before she could stop them. She raked her fingers through her hair, wondering how she looked. "I mean, I was thinking about last night." She wanted to crawl into a hole, but he didn't seem to notice her discomfort. He wore a white shirt, collar undone, and dress pants. It struck her that he must have come directly from work. He looked wonderful and she had to force herself to look away.

"May I come in?"

"Yes, of course." She was still clutching a paintbrush. "Just let me deal with this and I'll make us a cup of tea." She hesitated. "That is, if you'd like one."

"Sounds good." He followed her down the hall and watched her clean her brushes, his presence filling the studio. He nodded toward the easel. "May I look?"

"There's not much to see, but okay." What was she doing? She usually *hated* having people look at her work before it was completed. And yet it seemed like the most natural thing in the world to be sharing the new project with him.

He studied her work, glancing back and forth between the original sketch and the emerging painting. Looking up, he caught her watching him and he nodded, a slow smile lighting his eyes. "This is going to be a great painting."

She came to his side carrying two mugs and he

accepted his wordlessly. "I like it so far, but I'll know a bit better in a few days."

"That's what I came to talk to you about . . . a few days."

"A few days?" He wasn't making any sense.

"Yes." He seemed to be enjoying himself. "Come on—let's sit outside and enjoy the sun." They went outside. "Where do you usually sit?"

She gave him a lopsided grin. "I have all this deck furniture, but my favorite spot is the top step of the stairs leading down to the beach."

"All right. It's a bit damp, but let's use these." He grabbed a couple of cushions and placed them side by side on the step. "Now you get settled and I'll be right back. I have something for you." He balanced his mug on the railing and went back into the house.

He was back moments later. "Okay now, close your eyes." She complied and heard him sit down beside her.

"Wait a minute." She smiled as a familiar scent wafted past her nose. "That smells like violets." She opened her eyes and he handed her an exquisite little bouquet of violets. Tears burned the backs of her eyes and she lowered her head, pretending to smell the flowers. "They're lovely," she said, her voice clogged with emotion, wishing that she could tell him that they were more precious to her than any arrangement she'd ever been given. "But why?"

"Why?" He looked into her eyes. She wanted to look away, to prevent him from reading her thoughts, but she couldn't. "Because I thought you'd enjoy them." He leaned forward, and for the first time seemed tentative. "You *do* like them, don't you?"

She nodded. "I love them," she said simply.

"Actually, I had another reason for coming to see you, but I didn't want to arrive empty-handed." He shot her a boyish grin, lightening the mood. "I came to ask you if you'd like to go sailing on Thursday. I'm hoping we might get to see some orcas."

"I'd love that, but don't you have to work?"

"Not to worry. I know the boss." He grinned.

"Well in that case, did you have any particular destination in mind?"

"I thought we'd head up toward Johnstone Strait. It's supposed to be the best place in the world to observe orcas." His eyes glowed as he warmed to his subject and Ashley felt the familiar lurch in her chest as he smiled down at her. "We probably won't make it that far in one day, but we have a good chance of seeing some migrating pods." Honey had wiggled into the small space between them and he scratched behind her ears. "I didn't think you'd want to stay overnight and leave Honey alone again." His eyes held hers. "Maybe some other time."

"Yeah," she said softly. It seemed like a feeble response, but she couldn't think of anything else to say.

"Good, that's settled then. I'll ask Betty to make us a picnic lunch." He rose and offered his hand, pulling her to her feet. "I'd better get going. Caity and I are going over her checklist tonight to make sure she has everything she needs for camp."

* * *

". . . and when they lie on the bottom of the pool you can hardly see them," said Caitlin, standing beside Ashley's easel the next morning. True to her word, the child had telephoned to ask if she could ride over for a visit. "They're the size of minnows, or maybe smaller, and I already looked them up in my book."

"That sounds like quite a book." Ashley smiled at the child.

"Daddy got it for me. It's called a reference book. He says he'll take me to Parksville later on this summer and we can look for sand dollars." She squatted down and wrapped her arms around Honey. "Honey would like it there. When the tide goes out you can walk for miles on the sand."

"Speaking of beaches, would you like to go down to the beach again? I'm working on a surprise painting for your dad and I'd like to do some more work on it." Ashley lifted out the canvas and Caitlin looked at it, her eyes lighting up.

"That's the one of Honey and me, down on your beach."

Ashley gathered up her painting supplies. "Yes, and I'm hoping to finish it today. I hate to ask you to not to tell your Dad, but since it's a present I think it would be okay if you kept it to yourself for a few days. Do you think you can keep it a secret?"

Caitlin nodded. "Presents are much better when they're a surprise." She held her hand out to the dog. "Come on, Honey, we're going to be in a painting."

The morning passed quickly and Ashley was pleased

with the results. She had captured Caitlin looking into the small pool, the dog beside her, head cocked. Looking at it critically, she decided that it was almost corny—and it would have been if the subject matter hadn't been so personal. Privately, she felt that it portrayed the joy and wonder of discovery, much as she herself was feeling with Matt.

She glanced across the beach to where Caity was having a serious one-sided conversation with Honey, and her heart filled with love for the young girl. She didn't know how Matt had been able to raise such an unspoiled child, but he'd done an amazing job. Caitlin looked up and gave Ashley a small wave, then ran across the beach. She stood beside Ashley's chair, one hand on her hip, studying the painting. "Look at Honey," she said, her voice wondrous. "She looks like she hears something."

Ashley smoothed the child's hair. "It does, doesn't it? I think it turned out quite well."

Caitlin nodded soberly and leaned against Ashley. "Me too." She was quiet for a moment. "I'm going to miss you while I'm at camp." She pulled away, her gaze steady. "I'm going to miss you a lot."

Ashley swallowed. "I'll miss you too. But guess what? You're going to be having so much fun it'll be over before you know it." She stood up and gathered her materials. "I have some ice cream today. Shall we go and get some?" The child's hand slipped into hers and they walked up the steps to the house, trailed by the little dog.

* * *

The house seemed empty after Caitlin went home. Ashley turned on the television for company and sat down, listlessly eating a salad. It was a relief when the phone rang.

"Hi! I hope I didn't get you away from anything." Gloria's voice was cheerful as usual. "Just thought I'd let you know we're having our first planning session on Friday evening at the community hall. Can you make it?"

"I sure can. Shall I bring anything?"

"No, just your enthusiasm. The meeting starts at seven, but if you can make it a bit before, I'll introduce you around."

"Will do. See you then."

"What a glorious day for a sail." Ashley glanced up at the blue sky as she drove across the island.

The housekeeper directed her to the side of the house. "The path down to the dock is over there. I've packed you a nice lunch, and he's waiting for you."

Ashley paused at the head of the ramp. The rising summer breeze caressed her face and she turned her face toward the sun. It promised to be a hot day on land, but the temperature on the water would be perfect. She'd tucked her hair underneath a baseball cap, not wanting to have to deal with strands of hair all day. It made her feel young and carefree and she ran lightly down to the dock.

Matt looked up and waved. "You look like a kid in that getup." He looked at her approvingly.

Ashley looked down at her cutoffs and tennis shoes.

"You're right—I do. I used to wear something like this when we sailed on English Bay. I hope it's okay, 'cause it's all I have with me."

"You look fine to me." His eyes crinkled. "Stow your bag down below if you like. I'm going to get under way."

"Let me know if you want any help," she said, settling onto a cushion at the stern. Matt was slowly pulling out of the bay under power, his hand light and sure on the wheel. While he was occupied, she allowed herself the luxury of looking at him. Standing with legs apart, he moved as one with the boat. Faded cutoffs hugged his thighs, revealing tanned, strongly muscled legs. As they got under way, the breeze toyed with his hair but he ignored it, pleasure radiating from his eyes. She glanced back toward the island, where Matt's home was barely visible among the tall cedars. Between the boat and the shore, a pair of cormorants flew by on rapid wingbeats, and she gave herself over to the pleasure of being on the water again.

"Penny for your thoughts." Matt's voice broke into her reverie.

She hitched up one leg beneath her and turned to face him. "I wish I could tell you that they were deep and profound, but I was just letting my mind drift." She looked away hesitantly, aware that he was waiting for her to speak. "My life has changed since I moved here; my world has shifted around." Her gaze returned to him as she spoke. "And I like it."

It had been several days since he'd brought her the violets. She'd been working steadily, but during the inevitable quiet moments, she'd missed his company. Her eyes lingered on his sensuous mouth and she experienced a quick pang of jealousy at the thought of him dating other women. Pulling down the brim of her cap she looked out to open water, silently scolding herself for having negative thoughts on such a perfect day. After all, he was with her now. It was their day to enjoy, and she intended to do just that.

"If you'll take over the wheel for a couple of minutes I'll run up some canvas," he said, breaking in on her thoughts. His hand brushed against hers and her heart quickened at the brief contact. "We'll be in open water for a while, so don't be surprised if I don't say much."

Within minutes the jib and the mainsail had caught the breeze and the boat surged ahead, cutting eagerly through the water. Ashley watched Matt's masterful handling and she laughed aloud, all negative thoughts dashed away by the fresh saltwater spray. He moved with a fluid grace, his movements economical and confident as he guided the boat steadily toward their destination. Ashley scrambled to comply with his infrequent commands, and they worked comfortably together, the hours seeming like minutes.

Sailing into a cluster of small islands, the boat slowed. "I've often seen orcas through here," he said, "so keep your eyes peeled."

Ashley looked around. Apart from the spectacular scenery, there didn't seem to be anything different about this area. "Why here?"

"Because it's a main highway for both the transient and the resident pods. The salmon come through here for their spawning runs and then there's the attraction of the rubbing beaches in Johnstone Strait."

"Rubbing beaches?" The sails went slack and she looked up, startled.

"This looks like a good place to stop for lunch," he said. "I'll just drop sail and toss out the anchor." He grinned at her. "Do you mind getting out the picnic basket? I'm starving."

Three small islands formed a small, semicircular shelter, and within minutes the boat rode at anchor in the clear green water.

"Coffee?" Ashley held the thermos above a cup. "It smells heavenly."

"I'd love one." Matt folded his long frame into a canvas chair and stretched out his long legs. "I see you found the folding table and chairs."

"Couldn't miss them." She smiled at him, almost giddy with happiness. "Thanks for leaving them out."

"Caught in the act," he said, not sounding at all contrite. "Now, where were we? Ah yes, you were asking about rubbing beaches." He took a swallow of coffee. "Robson Bight has shallow waters with a pebble bottom, and orcas are often seen there rubbing their bodies on the pebbles. Nobody knows why they do it, but of course there are lots of theories."

"Maybe it just feels good." Ashley frowned. "Where is Robson Bight?"

"Sorry. It's another name for Johnstone Strait."

Ashley shook her head. "There's so much to learn. I've only recently learned that we have more than one kind of orca up here."

"Actually, there are three, and they each have unique eating habits." He eyed the fried chicken. "Speaking of eating, do you mind if I dig in?"

"No, of course not. I think I'll have some too." She helped herself to a piece of chicken and some salad.

Chapter Nine

"Mmmm. Betty makes the best fried chicken," he said, wiping his fingers on a napkin. "So. We have resident orcas. That's pretty self-explanatory. They travel in pods of between 6 to 50 and range up to 800 kilometers up and down the coast of B.C. and into the Strait of Juan de Fuca, feeding primarily on salmon. The second type, the transients, can range up to 1450 kilometers from Alaska to California, and travel in much smaller pods. In addition to salmon they eat seals, whales, and sea birds. Then there are the offshore orcas. They live in the open ocean and eat only fish."

Ashley looked at him thoughtfully. "You know a lot about this. What piqued your interest?"

He shrugged self-consciously. "I don't know." His eyes grew distant. "No, that's not true. I do know. I'd just started to make enough money to think about buying a home and Emily and I were on the ferry, coming over to Madrona. We were thinking about buying a place on the island. Anyway, that was the first time I saw an orca. It was out in Georgia Strait, and it was spy-hopping." He paused and looked at her, as though eager to share the experience. "You know how you see them do that on the nature specials on television?" She nodded and he continued. "Well, I saw one doing that and I swear it was looking toward the ferry, wondering why we were invading its territory. I've never seen that behavior since then, but from that moment I decided to try to learn as much as I could about them." He spread his hands. "As an amateur, of course."

"From what I heard when you and Jessica were talking, more people should learn about them. Then maybe we wouldn't foul up their environment." She reached for the thermos containing the coffee. "Have you learned anything bad about them? Anything negative?"

He shook his head. "No. And I get so angry when people call them 'killer whales.' Do they kill to eat? Absolutely, but we can't expect them to starve." He gave a short, mirthless laugh. "Trust man to criticize an animal. Man, who wages war and kills millions."

He held out his mug. "Don't let me get started, Ashley. I'd be farther ahead to stay focused on the orcas. At least that's one area where I might have a chance of making a difference."

He stood up and stretched, eyes scanning the water. "Well, I didn't expect the orcas to show up just because we came out, but I was hoping we'd see some today." He leaned against the gunwale, long legs braced against the gentle roll. "I wanted to share them with you."

She was touched by the words. "Thank you, Matt. That would have been wonderful, but just bringing me here is the best birthday gift you could have given me." The moment the words were out she turned away, wishing she could take them back.

He looked instantly contrite. "I didn't know it was your birthday."

Ashley blushed furiously, waving her hands in front of her face. "No, no. I don't even know why I said that. It's not for a couple of days." She fussed with the picnic basket, avoiding those probing eyes.

Matt came up behind her and took her gently by the shoulders, turning her around. Lifting her chin, he gazed into her eyes. "What is it, Ashley? You're upset about something, and I'm pretty sure you're not one of those women who worries every time another birthday comes around." He brushed a stray strand of hair away from her face. "So what is it?"

She pulled away and looked up into his eyes "Am I so transparent?" She gathered her thoughts. "It just occurred to me that I won't be seeing Jessica on my birthday. For as many years as I can remember, we've shared each other's birthday. This is the first time we've lived in different towns, and to make it worse, she's working out of town and she won't be back until late Saturday night." She squared her shoulders. "Sorry if I sound self-indulgent. I knew I'd miss her when I moved, and that there might be some lonely days, but the truth is, it hasn't been so bad."

"You're lucky to have such a good friend."

"I sure am." She brightened. "And I forgot to tell

you. I'm going to get involved with the Little Theater group."

"So! Brenda got to you, did she? What does she have lined up for you, or do you know yet?"

"I'm going to help with the set painting. It'll be fun to learn something new." She reclaimed her chair and he sat again, opposite her. "We're having our first meeting tomorrow evening at the community center." She looked at him hopefully. "I don't suppose you have time to get involved yourself?"

"No, but I help with the advertising costs and the program. It's not as personal as giving my time, but Brenda assures me that every little bit is appreciated."

"I'm sure she understands that you're a busy guy." Relieved to be on a less emotional topic, Ashley patted her stomach. "When Betty packs a picnic she goes all out. I won't need to eat again for a week."

Matt's eyes softened. "Caity and I are lucky to have her. She takes good care of us."

"Oh, I almost forgot to ask you. Did she get away okay?" Ashley leaned closer. "She came to visit me the other day."

"So I heard." Matt chuckled. "Yes, she got away. Bouncing off the walls with excitement one minute and worried about me the next." His face turned pensive. "It's quiet around the house without her, but camp is good for her."

"Will you be doing the market in her place this weekend?"

"Nope. That was our agreement from the get-go. I promised to help, but I made it clear that if she wanted time off, I wouldn't do the market for her." He shook his head. "It's her project, and it has to stay that way." He turned to Ashley, one eyebrow raised. "Do you think that's too harsh?"

"Absolutely not. I admire you for sticking to your guns." Her eyes roamed over his face, lingering on the line of his jaw. "We all have to set limits, I guess. Speaking of which, Jessica called me last week and quoted from an article that mentioned you. It made you sound tough but fair." She paused. "Sort of like a cross between Mother Teresa and Warren Buffett."

"Well, it's difficult to run a company of any kind without being labeled tough at one time or another." He looked amused. "So, your friend was checking up on me, was she? Did she find anything else?"

"Let's see." Ashley bit her lower lip, wishing she'd never brought it up. "As I recall, most of what she read to me was glowing."

He lowered his head, mouth twitching in a smile. "That's me all over, just a nice guy." He scanned the water again. "Too bad about the orcas, but maybe another time." He stood up and glanced at his watch. "If you don't mind putting the lunch away, I'll winch up the anchor. We can run north for another half hour or so and then we'll turn back." He grinned boyishly. "Are you up for some more work?"

She lifted a hand to the brim of her cap. "Aye, aye, Captain."

They rounded the group of islands and turned back south, spurred on by a steady wind. They had just passed the south end of the island group when Matt gestured excitedly to Ashley, calling her to his side. "Orcas," he said, "there, off the port side." The whales were traveling rapidly, following the route they'd taken earlier in the day. A black dorsal fin sliced through the water, then several more, surrounding a smaller one. It was difficult to judge the number in the group, but there appeared to be eight, and they watched in awe as the magnificent creatures passed within fifty yards of the boat. It seemed perfectly natural to be standing beside Matt, his arm around her waist, and they followed the progress of the whales in silence until they disappeared from sight.

"You sure know how to show a girl a good time," she said, smiling up at him.

"I do my best," he drawled, giving her a quick squeeze. "Prepare to come about."

The afternoon passed too quickly; before she knew it Ashley was helping to stow away the last of the gear. The trees cast long shadows across Matt's property as they climbed wearily to his house.

"Would you like to stay for dinner? We could rustle up something, or we still have lots left over from lunch."

"I wouldn't mind just sitting down and having something cold." Ashley accompanied him into the house, and once again she marveled at the comfortable atmosphere of the sprawling home. "If you'll just show me where I can freshen up, I'll be right with you."

She reappeared a few minutes later, hair brushed and caught back with a ribbon she'd stuffed in her bag. Matt was about to slice a lemon and stopped, knife poised in the air.

"You look lovely," he said, abandoning the knife and moving toward her. There was no doubt about what he intended and her breath caught in her throat as he pulled her toward him, pinning her with his gaze. His lips captured hers and for a brief, incandescent moment she leaned into him, a ripple of pleasure dancing down her spine.

"I've wanted to do that all day," he said huskily, brushing his lips against hers one more time before releasing her.

"Can't say I didn't think of it a couple of times myself." She reached up to wipe a smudge of lipstick from his face. "But it was worth waiting for."

They sat side by side on the deck, peacefully watching fishing boats and pleasure boats returning from a day on the water. Held in the magic spell they had woven during the day, neither felt the need to talk. The sun sank lower behind the tall trees, sending fingers of shadow across the deck. Suddenly chilled, Ashley rubbed her arms then pulled her hand away, surprised to find that she had a slight sunburn.

"Are you all right?" Matt's concern was immediate.

"I'm fine." She swung around to face him. "Just a touch of sunburn, but it's a small price to pay for such a wonderful day."

"I have some lotion. . . ."

"No, it's fine." She reached out and took his hand. "I plan to finish a couple of paintings tomorrow, so I think I'll head home and get a good night's sleep."

Matt squeezed her hand, then stood up, drawing her

up with him. "I hate to see you go, but I brought home a report to study." His face turned serious. "I'm on a board that's meeting next week and I'm at odds with a few of the other directors on the decision we have to make." He seemed to be looking inward, and Ashley caught a glimpse of the businessman beneath the casual exterior. "I want to be sure of all my facts before I weigh in with my opinion."

He draped his arm around her shoulder and they walked outside to her van. "Here we are again, saying good-bye at my place."

Ashley's eyes shone as she raised her lips. "But we're getting pretty good at it, aren't we?" He kissed her deeply in reply, and they held each other for a long time before she turned and climbed into her vehicle. As she pulled out, she rolled down her window. "Thanks again, Matt. See you soon."

"Oh, you can count on it, my sweet," he said as the van disappeared from sight. "You can count on it."

Ashley stepped back from her easel, studying the painting of the old farmhouse surrounded by the apple orchard. She had just added her signature, a process she always saved for last. *It's not the best thing I've ever done,* she thought critically, *but it's good.* She set it aside, thinking about what type of frame would show it to its best advantage. Maybe she would leave this one to Gabrielle's innate sense of what was right.

Humming happily to herself, she placed the canvas of Caitlin and Honey on the easel and looked at it with fresh eyes. It was good, and she felt a warm glow knowing the pleasure Matt would get from it. Very little remained to be done and she settled down to add the final touches. An hour later she added a discreet *A. Stewart* to the bottom right-hand corner and stood back to survey the finished work. She had captured Caitlin squatting with one hand on each knee, peering down into the small tidal pool, Honey at her side, head cocked as though listening. The effect was so charming that Ashley couldn't help but smile. She would leave the choice of frame to Matt, and decided to give it to him on their next meeting.

The lights were on and quite a few cars were already parked outside the community center when Ashley arrived that evening. Unlike many of the public buildings on the island, this one was fairly new, and she could see at a glance that it had been designed as a multipurpose structure. Entering hesitantly, she poked her head into the main hall. Chairs had been drawn up in a loose circle near the stage and were occupied by people who seemed to be catching up on one another's news. Brenda noticed her and waved a hand, beckoning her forward. "Here's Ashley," she said to the group, introducing her to each individual in turn. She was warmly received, and concentrated on remembering as many names as possible. Gloria jumped up and pulled another chair from a stack, motioning Ashley to come and sit down between Fran and her.

She smiled her thanks, then turned to Fran. "I understand you'll be showing me the ins and outs of set painting."

Fran crinkled her nose, trying to prevent her glasses from sliding off. "I'll tell you everything I've learned, such as it is." Her eyes sparkled. "Ever since I read for the director a couple of weeks ago and they told me I got the part, I've been a nervous wreck." She bobbed her head. "But I've decided it's time to come out from behind the scenes and try some acting, you know?"

Ashley smiled. "I have a feeling you're going to be great."

The informal meeting was called to order and everyone received a printed schedule. Ashley was surprised at the extensive planning that had already taken place, and at the hundreds of details to be coordinated before the production would be presented to the public. She listened attentively as questions were asked and answered. Brenda would handle advertising, promotion, and ticket sales again this year. Ashley would be working closely with the set design and property people, and they broke off into a separate group to discuss the set layout, and what they would need to create the desired effects. The discussion was fascinating and she was startled when they were called to rejoin the others for coffee. Her group hastily agreed to get together at the local coffee shop in a few days and finalize their plans.

She walked into the well-equipped kitchen, where someone had laid out mugs and some chunky oatmeal cookies. As she was adding cream to her coffee, the director wandered in, papers threatening to escape from the file folder held precariously under his arm. His glasses were perched on top of his head and he peered at her somewhat myopically.

"I wanted to say that I am a great admirer of your work." He seemed painfully shy, and she smiled at him kindly. "I wish you would do another calendar," he continued. "That last one was absolutely spectacular." He sidled toward the coffee urn, and Ashley set down her cup.

"Here, let me get some coffee for you. You're about to lose your papers." She filled a cup for him, and stirred in the two lumps of sugar he indicated. "I enjoyed doing that calendar, but it took a lot of time, and I must confess I dislike working to a deadline. As for this . . ." She waved her hand toward the rest of the group. "This is going to be pure fun, and I'll enjoy the interaction with other people for a change."

He nodded his head, and they went back out into the middle of a heated discussion.

". . . Well I know what I heard!" Roger Butler, the set carpenter, leaned forward aggressively, finger and thumb held close together. "They've been lobbying the government for years to lift the moratorium on oil and gas exploration and they're this close to succeeding." He became more agitated, his voice rising. "Back in 1972 our federal government did something right when the ban on oil tanker traffic and exploration was imposed. But thanks to growing demands for oil and aggressive lobbying they were about to reverse themselves in 1986."

"I remember reading about that." Brenda looked around at the others. "I was terrified."

"And with good reason." Roger stood up, started pacing. "But then the Exxon Valdez oil spill happened and they knew there'd be too much of a public outcry if they tried to slip that one past the public. So here we are, more than twenty years later and they're trying again. They're even talking about oil tankers up the Inside Passage. It's madness, pure madness."

Ashley could scarcely believe her ears.

"Yeah, I also read about this." Lars Christensen nodded vigorously. "Back then—in 1972—they were quick to respond to the Alaska pipeline. They were all in favor of protecting the environment then, so why are they turning a blind eye now? We're talking about some of the most pristine environment in the world."

Roger made a rude sound. "Tell that to the oil exploration companies. They don't give a damn. All they care about is the bottom line." He sat back down, as if in defeat. "What we need is someone on our side."

Ashley sipped her coffee thoughtfully, listening as the others gave their opinions. The notion of an oil platform, with all its attendant equipment and traffic was unthinkable. She closed her eyes and pictured the pod of orcas she'd seen just yesterday. Orcas had been migrating in these waters for thousands of years; the implications were unacceptable. The group's outrage flowed around her, and she felt an urgent need to find out if the reports were true.

On the way home, images of sparkling ocean, tall old-growth forests, and shiny black orca bodies breaking the surface flickered through her mind like images in a nature special. But the sound track was wrong; instead of soaring music she heard Roger's voice, harsh and angry as he railed against the possibility of offshore oil and gas exploration.

"What would Jessica do?" she asked herself, then gave herself a mental slap. "Of course," she said aloud, the first faint hope appearing on the horizon. "This is Jessica's bread and butter."

Barely acknowledging Honey's greeting, she punched in Jessica's number in her speed dial as soon as she got home.

"Jessica Burns."

Ashley sank down into a chair, relieved to hear the familiar voice. "Oh, Jess, I'm so glad to hear your voice."

"Hello, stranger." Jessica's confident voice was a much-needed tonic. "What's up? You sound distracted."

"I am, Jess. You won't believe this. I just heard the most upsetting rumor. Now that's all it is, just a rumor, but I'm hoping you can use your contacts and, you know, check it out." She knew she was babbling but she couldn't help it.

"Whoa! Hold on." Ashley could picture her friend holding up a hand. "Now let's start again. Nice and slow. What's this all about?"

As calmly as possible, Ashley filled her in on the discussion that had taken place at the community center. "It sounds like your kind of story, Jess. But even if you can't use it, could you at least find out if it's true?"

"I hate to say this, Ashley, but it could be one hundred percent true. I heard a few weeks ago that the government was slashing import duties on offshore drilling equipment. You know, making it easier to bring it in from other countries." She paused. "They wouldn't be doing that without a reason."

Ashley absorbed this information. "You're right. It

doesn't sound good. Oh, Jess, if only you could have been with us yesterday. Matt and I sailed up toward Johnstone Strait. I had no idea the scenery was so breathtaking up there. And on the way back we saw a group, or I should say a pod, of orcas. Now if that isn't a sign, what is?"

"Back up, kiddo. Did you say you were out sailing with Matt yesterday? You have to keep your Auntie Jessica up-to-date on these things, you know."

Ashley felt herself relax. "Oh, it's good to talk to you, Jess. You always make me laugh." She closed her eyes. "We had a wonderful day. It was sunny, and the wind was just right for sailing. His housekeeper made us a picnic and we stopped in the lee of some islands and had the most relaxing lunch. We were the only boat in the area, except for a small group of kayakers." She sighed. "It was perfect."

"This is beginning to sound serious, Ash. Have you been seeing much of him?" Her friend's voice held notes of curiosity mixed in with concern.

"Quite a bit, I guess. But I wouldn't say it's serious yet. We're both fairly tentative at this point, and that's just fine with me, but without a doubt he's the most appealing man I've ever known."

"I can understand why you feel that way. He has something about him, doesn't he?" Ashley murmured her agreement and Jessica carried on. "And he's easy on the eyes. What about his daughter?"

"She's away at camp right now. She visits me often, but to be honest I think Honey is the main attraction, not me. Anyway, she's decided she wants to be a marine biologist."

"Yeah, well, that's this week. Next week it'll be something else. Listen, Ashley, I'm happy for you, but go slow, okay?"

"I will, Jess, and thanks for listening. Will you call me if you dig up anything?"

"You can count on it. Look, kiddo, did they by any chance have the name of the company?"

"Did I forget to tell you that? Shows how upset I am. It's called La Perouse Exploration."

"Leave it with me, and Ashley . . ."

"Yes?"

"Happy birthday tomorrow."

Ashley smiled to herself as she puttered around getting ready for bed. If anyone could get to the bottom of this, it would be Jessica.

Ashley pulled the duvet up over her head, trying to block out the persistent ringtone. The sound reminded her of her conversation with Jessica and she swung her feet over the side of the bed and fumbled for the phone.

"Good morning, birthday girl." Matt's voice raised the fine hairs on the back of her neck and she was suddenly awake. "How soon can you be ready?"

Ashley groaned. "Ready for what?" She flopped back down on the bed. "You woke me up," she grouched, trying unsuccessfully to sound annoyed. It wasn't easy with a picture of Matt's engaging smile hovering in her mind.

He laughed, and a delicious tingling sensation worked its way up from her toes. "You, my dear, are going on a birthday adventure. I'll pick you up in half an hour."

"What?" she sputtered. "Where are we going?" The thought of spending her birthday with him was appealing, but . . . "At least give me a hint of what kind of clothes to put on."

"Don't tempt me," he said with a low growl, and her stomach did a little flip-flop. "But to answer your question, be casual and comfortable. It could be a long day."

"You're impossible." She was starting to get into the spirit of the surprise. "I don't know if I can be ready in half an hour, though. I need to shower, walk Honey, and . . ."

"Details, details. I'll be there in half an hour, and if you're not ready, I'll wait for you. After all, you're the star attraction today."

Ashley couldn't stop smiling as she showered. Matt had a way of making their time together very special. She thought back to Jessica's cautionary words the night before. It was hard to go slowly when there was such a strong attraction building between them. Matt felt it too, she mused, scanning the outfits in her closet. Holding up a long flared skirt, she swirled in front of the mirror and decided it would be as good as anything. She topped it with a simple tank top and a light, long-sleeved blouse tied at the waist. With her hair pulled back and tied with a ribbon she was ready to face the day.

Darting back to the bedroom she chose some matching earrings, pausing to check the effect in the mirror. The young woman with the shining eyes who gazed back was scarcely recognizable as the same one who'd entered this house just a few short weeks before.

*   *   *

Ashley was walking Honey in the driveway when Matt arrived. Shading her eyes from the sun, she drank in the sight of him as though she'd been away from him for months. His long legs ate up the space between them and then there he was, standing in front of her.

"Happy birthday, Ashley." Blue eyes searched her face and she gazed back at him, the dog forgotten for the moment. "You look lovely this morning." With a slow, deliberate movement, he lowered his head, brushing her lips with his own. Her eyes remained fixed on his, and as he pulled away she detected a flash of desire. It lasted for a brief, intense moment and then he tore his eyes away and looked down at Honey. "Will she be all right for the day?" he asked, leaning over to pet her.

"Yes, she'll be fine. She's one of those rare dogs who'll use a litter box if she has to." Ashley called the dog into the house, where she curled up in her basket in the studio. Spotting the painting she'd done for Matt, she hesitated, then picked it up and brought it outside. "It may be my birthday, but I have a gift for you." Her eyes were shining as she turned the canvas around to display the painting. "It isn't framed because I thought you'd want to choose your own."

He stared at it then looked at her, a small frown appearing on his forehead. "You did this for me?" The expression of wonder on his face grew as he examined it more closely. "It's amazing." He tilted his head to one side, lost in the picture. "It captures them both perfectly."

He continued to admire the painting as she locked up the house, a delighted expression on his face. "I think I'll wait for a while before I get it framed," he said, settling her into the vehicle. He laid the painting in the back, and pulled out of the driveway. Reaching across the front seat, he gripped Ashley's hand. "Thank you. That's the best gift I've ever been given."

She smiled to herself as he headed across the island. It had been worth the effort to see the expression on his face. And today . . . well, now that she was awake she could hardly wait to see what he had up his sleeve.

Matt pulled through the gates of his property. The helicopter crouched on the pad, and the same pilot stood in the sunshine, talking with Archie. "Madam, your carriage awaits," he said with a flourish, guiding her toward the helicopter. He settled her into the front seat, with a quick explanation that birthday girls always got to ride up front. Within no time they were airborne, leaving the island behind.

Below them, boats of all sizes dotted the Strait of Georgia. She observed them with fresh eyes, newly aware of the large freighters heading toward the Port of Vancouver. In the distance, to her left, she could see the route she and Matt had taken in the sailboat only two days before. She wondered if she should inform him about the disturbing rumor she'd heard at the community center, but as quickly as the notion came into her head she decided against it. Jessica would get back to her soon enough, and she could share her information at that time.

Comfortable with her decision, she settled back to enjoy the short trip. Within a few minutes they were approaching the mainland, but she was surprised when they veered away from Richmond, where Matt's building was located. Instead, they headed to the airport, landing well away from the main terminal. Matt helped her out of the helicopter and into a motorized cart. Following the painted lines on the tarmac, they drove up to a waiting private jet, where a steward greeted them.

"It's good to see you again, sir," he said with a professional smile. "The crew is all aboard and we've been cleared for takeoff in five minutes."

Chapter Ten

Ashley mounted the steps and settled into a wide leather seat across from Matt. A low coffee table separated them and she took in her surroundings, trying to appear casual as the aircraft taxied to the runway. They were given clearance almost immediately, and she was aware that Matt was watching her with a satisfied smile on his face. If he was trying to surprise her, he was doing a good job. She glanced toward the rear of the aircraft, where the steward was busying himself, then leaned forward, speaking in a low voice. "Am I acting cool enough? Because I'm definitely impressed."

"You're supposed to be. After all, it's your birthday." He looked up as the steward approached with orange juice, coffee, and delicate pastries. "Thank you, Glenn. We can manage for ourselves."

Ashley glanced out the window. "Where are we going, or is it a secret?"

"I'm taking you to lunch." He leaned forward and poured two cups of coffee. "In the Okanagan. And after lunch I have a surprise for you."

"You mean this isn't enough of a surprise?" She picked up the cup and took a sip. The coffee smelled great and tasted even better. "Will we get to see your family's winery?"

He nodded. "Yup. We'll be landing in Oliver in about thirty-five minutes. It's the closest airstrip to the winery."

She returned her gaze to the scenery below. The Coast Mountains still held pockets of snow, and high mountain lakes reflected the blue of the sky. Forested slopes gradually gave way to a broad valley. Sunlight glinted off lakes, and the bottom of the valley was lush and green, while the hills on either side were dry and dotted with clusters of ponderosa pines. The aircraft started its descent and she leaned forward eagerly. "It looks like a desert down there," she observed. "I spent a few weeks here one summer when I was about twelve, but I'd forgotten what it's like."

"Left alone it *would* be a desert." Matt looked out as a patchwork of orchards came into sight. "It's amazing what can be accomplished with irrigation." Every available space in the valley bottoms and up the hills on either side was taken up with some form of agriculture. Old cherry trees spread their gnarled branches, contrasting dramatically with the small, neat trees of the new intensively planted orchards. The effect was a pleasing mixture and Ashley wished that she could see more as the aircraft touched down.

The steps swung down and heat invaded the cabin. Matt exited first and turned, offering her his hand. "We're not in Kansas anymore," he said with a smile and she silently agreed as they crossed the tarmac to an open-air Jeep. The cool greens and ocean breezes of Madrona Island seemed a lifetime away.

"I asked the family not to meet us so I could give you a quick tour of the town." A key was in the ignition and he turned it, a sheepish grin on his face. "I don't want to share you any more than is necessary today."

Ashley laughed, secretly pleased. They drove the few miles into the small town, which faintly resembled a movie set. Old buildings lined the main street, and a sprawling high school overlooked the town, its spacious lawns bare of students in the summer hiatus. Matt pointed out the meandering oxbows of the river, where he and his high school friends had fished for carp, and the road to Mount Baldy, where he'd learned to ski. The tour was short, and they were soon driving south, passing countless orchards, broken only by fields of tomatoes and peppers.

"If Caitlin saw these tomatoes already ripening, she'd be jealous."

Matt reached over and covered her hand with his. "Funny, I was thinking the same thing." He pointed to a glint of water in the distance. "That's Osoyoos Lake, where I learned to sail."

Ashley sat up and peered ahead; it was hard to take everything in. Matt slowed the Jeep and turned onto a side road, which meandered through a large hay field and across the bottom of the valley. Horses grazed in fields along the road, tails swatting at flies. At a suitable vantage point he stopped the car and pointed to the hills on the opposite side of the valley. From here they appeared to be covered in green corduroy.

"Those are the family vineyards," he said, and Ashley could hear the pride in his voice. "That side of the valley has been almost entirely replanted with grapes in the past ten years."

She shaded her eyes. Acres of vineyards hugged the contours of the hillside, stretching as far as the cliffs in the distance. Up and down the valley, row upon row of precisely spaced vines gleamed in the sunlight. "That's a *lot* of grapes," she murmured.

Matt nodded and pulled back onto the narrow road. "You can say that again. It's a lot of work too, but Dad says he couldn't imagine himself doing anything else." He shook his head. "Mom complains that she can hardly get him to come inside for dinner at night."

Ashley pulled her eyes away from the mesmerizing rows of grapes. "How many acres do you have altogether?"

"We have three hundred and twenty acres, including the property the winery sits on." He turned up a steep hill and they were hit with a refreshing mist from an overhead sprinkler. "That's not a lot by some standards but Dad says it's the right size for him." Moisture dripped from the glistening leaves and bird boxes adorned posts at regular intervals along the road.

They turned toward a double row of poplars and Ashley's hand flew to her mouth. A graceful archway sat astride the driveway, ornately decorated with cast-metal vines and leaves. A simple sign in a flowing metal script hung from the arch.

"The Vineyard," she said, reading the sign. Then her eyes were drawn beyond the gates and into the shadowy green arcade of poplars. At the end of the driveway, a graceful stone structure greeted them, and her fingers itched to sketch it. "It's magical," she said, turning to him. "It looks like it belongs in Tuscany."

He smiled and drove slowly down the shaded drive, pulling up behind the main building. A smaller archway echoed the one on the driveway, welcoming visitors to the winery. Riotous flowerbeds encircled the building and Ashley stopped to admire some climbing hydrangea beside the front door.

The building was an oasis of cool in the summer heat. Dark wooden floors softened their steps, and Ashley peeked into a room devoted to wine tasting and retail sales. Glasses gleamed in the subdued light and racks of bottles nestled against the walls. Beyond the sales area, a spacious foyer led to an inviting terrace that ran the length of the building. Grapevines grew among the open beams, shading tables from the direct sun. The entire front of the terrace overlooked the vineyards and the valley below. Ashley raised her eyebrows at the sight of the tables set with linen and sparkling glasses. Most of them were occupied.

"We offer a limited menu at lunchtime and into the afternoon. Evenings are for family, although Mom does break her own rule and accept private parties from time to time."

"Matthew. There you are." They turned to see an attractive woman coming toward them. Her long hair was pulled back in a soft bun at the back of her head, but it was her eyes that struck Ashley. They were the same blue as her son's and they sparkled with pleasure to see him. She held out her arms for a brief hug then turned to Ashley with a welcoming smile.

"Thank you for coming to visit us, Ashley. Matthew tells me it's your birthday today." She glanced quickly at her son.

"My goodness, I'd forgotten about that." Ashley looked around, taking in the details of the stone building. "Your place is very peaceful, Mrs. Ryan."

"Thank you my dear, but please, call me Sheila." She smiled graciously. "We've tried to make it that way. We want our visitors to have a memorable experience." Turning back to Matt, her eyes lit up. "And how is my granddaughter?"

"Same as ever. After she left for camp I discovered a list of things she wants me to do while she's away." He shook his head. "At the top of the list she informs me that I'm to check her garden twice a day." His voice softened. "She's really great. I'm proud of the way she's growing up."

"As well you should be. Now, I've saved you the corner table you requested." She led them to a table almost hidden behind a trellis of clematis. "I'll join you for coffee when you've finished your lunch. We're short-handed in the kitchen today, but the rush is almost over. By the way, your dad is working up at the north end of the property today. He said to tell you he'll see you for dinner."

With that, she disappeared in the direction of the kitchen and Matt watched her with a fond smile. "Well, what do you think so far?"

"It's like stepping into the pages of a travel magazine. And your mother is lovely." Resting her chin on her hand, she looked out over the vineyards. Sprinklers in the adjacent field sent spurts of water arcing high in the air, creating miniature rainbows above the vines. The place had a dreamlike quality, and not for the first time she sensed that it was too good to be true. Oh, but she hoped she was wrong!

Matt looked up from the menu and she couldn't stop the telltale flush that crept up her neck. Slightly flustered, she picked up her own menu and pretended to study it.

Matt's mother joined them as they sipped their coffee. "How was your lunch?"

"Excellent." And it had been—a simple shrimp salad served with hearts of romaine and drizzled with a mild curry dressing. "I was going to have some dessert, but I'm too full."

"I'm glad you enjoyed it. Matthew, your sister is working in the wine shop today. She was escorting a tour when you arrived, but she's looking forward to seeing you later." She stood up. "Well, I'll leave you two for now. Have fun this afternoon."

Ashley shot him a curious look. "Are you going to tell me what the surprise is?"

His eyes danced. "But if I did that, it wouldn't be a surprise, would it?"

"You're impossible, Matthew Ryan." Ashley looked

out over the valley. "You know, every time I look out there I see something different, something unique to this valley." Her voice turned thoughtful. "I could do a whole series of paintings up here. Everywhere I look I see something I'd like to capture. It's hard to take it all in."

"That's why I've arranged your birthday surprise," he said, holding her chair as she rose from the table. "Come on, we're due down in Osoyoos in half an hour."

They drove along the back roads and were descending into the valley bottom when they came upon a group of people inflating a hot-air balloon.

"Oh look!" cried Ashley. "A hot-air balloon. I've always wanted to go up in one of those."

Matt pulled into the field. "Happy birthday, Ashley. Let's go for a ride."

She looked from Matt to the balloon. Filling rapidly, the balloon rose into the air, a bold slash of color against the summer sky. "What a perfect surprise." She looked around. "Are we going up alone?"

"Just the two of us and the operator." He walked around the vehicle to help her out.

She almost stumbled as she climbed out of the Jeep, excitement making her clumsy. But Matt was there to catch her, and he kept his arm around her waist as they walked over to the balloon.

"Just a minute, folks." They turned to see a young woman with a camera. "If you'd like to stand beside the gondola, I'll take your picture." They laughingly complied, then stepped into the gondola for their instructions as the ground crew prepared to set them loose.

The balloon lifted silently into the air and Matt put

his arm around her waist once more, drawing her close. Ashley looked over the edge as they started to drift silently in the breeze, gaining altitude. Below them, the lake sparkled. "See there?" Matt pointed to a small marina on the west shore of the lake. "That's where I kept my first sailboat."

They drifted above lakefront homes and were soon looking down on peach and apple orchards. The pickers looked up and waved as they floated by, serenely quiet in their airborne transport. On either side of the valley, the hills rose, the sagebrush gray and sere in the summer heat.

"I feel like I'm floating on a cloud." Ashley gazed up into Matt's eyes. She leaned into his shoulder, contentment seeping through her body. *I'll remember this forever,* she told herself. *Even if nothing comes of this relationship, I'll always have this day.*

Matt pointed below. "Those are our vineyards." His eyes shone with pride.

Rows of vines hugged the undulating hillsides. "Now I can see the scope of the operation." She pointed to the parking lot, which was almost full. "Business is good today."

As they floated past the boundaries of the Ryan property the terrain turned rugged. The balloon operator pointed off to the side. "California bighorn sheep," he said, indicating the white-rumped animals perched on a rocky slope. A short distance away, another group munched on dry grass, looking up at the balloon with amber eyes.

The valley continued to unfold below them and

they followed the river for a few more miles before landing softly in another large field. "I could do it all over again," said Ashley, stepping regretfully out of the gondola.

"We will." Matt held her hand as they walked toward the Jeep, which had been driven from the field of departure. "We'll do it again soon."

Matt's sister was ringing up a sale when they reentered the winery, and was discussing the merits of the winery's Gewürztraminer wine. "Enjoy," she called as the couple left cradling their purchase.

"Hello, sis." Matt gathered Laura in a bear hug then stepped back, turning to Ashley. "Ashley, I'd like you to meet my bratty little sister, Laura."

Ashley stepped forward, smiling as Laura gave Matt a sisterly swat. "Don't listen to him, Ashley. It's a delight to meet you. How was your balloon ride?"

Ashley was immediately at home with Matt's tall, rangy sister. "It was fantastic, and a great way to see the countryside." She glanced around the room. "So, you do the tastings as well as the sales and the tours? That's a real handful."

Laura automatically straightened up a brochure rack. "We have a full-time staff, but I enjoy helping out during the summer rush."

At that moment more visitors arrived and Matt and Ashley quietly slipped out and wandered out onto the patio. Gravitating toward the railing, they stood side by side, their shoulders touching. The air was heavy with late-afternoon heat, but they were comfortable in the shade of the grape leaves.

"I feel like I'm in a fairy tale," said Ashley softly. "This has been an amazing day." She turned to find Matt looking at her and the longing in his eyes made her heart stand still. Picking up her hand, he placed a kiss in her palm and her nerve endings sizzled as she looked down at his golden head. He closed her fingers around the kiss and pulled her hand to his chest. "I hope to give you many more such days," he said, his voice low and husky. "Many more indeed."

Candles flickered in crystal holders as the family gathered on the terrace for dinner. Matt's father beamed his approval as Matt and Laura regaled Ashley with stories of their childhood. The family bonds were strong and supportive, and as they teased each other, it became clear to Ashley that this strong foundation was one of the factors that enabled Matt to enter the world of business with such confidence.

The meal was relaxed and leisurely, but it was over too soon. "I hate to break this up," said Matt, "but we have to be back at the airstrip at eight-thirty." He held Ashley's chair and she rose with a sigh.

"I wish I could stay right here," she said, feeling very much at home.

"You come back and visit us anytime." Laura gave her a sisterly hug, her eyes misty. "I haven't seen Matt looking so happy in a long time," she whispered as Matt shook hands with his father. "I hope we see you again."

Ashley closed her eyes and laid her head back on the comfortable seat as the jet rolled down the runway.

Was it just this morning that Matt had woken her? She opened her eyes to find him gazing at her.

"Did you have a good time today?" He leaned forward eagerly.

"The best," she said with a satisfied smile.

He fumbled in his jacket, extracting an envelope and moved to the seat beside her. "I thought you might like a souvenir. It's the picture from our balloon trip."

The picture was mounted on a folding card, the balloon operator's logo embossed in the corner. Ashley opened it slowly. The young photographer had captured them laughing, the colorful balloon straining toward the sky. He had his arm around her shoulder and she was leaning into him, truly happy for the first time in years.

The return trip was quick, and before they knew it they'd transferred to the helicopter. And then the dark hulk of the island appeared before them, soft lights spilling out from waterfront homes. On land, they ducked into the shelter of the house as the helicopter lifted off for the return trip to Vancouver.

"Would you care for something? A cup of tea?" Matt wandered into the kitchen, switching on the under-cabinet lighting.

"That would be great," said Ashley with a tired smile. "You know, to get me back down to earth." She leaned on the counter as he filled the kettle. His movements were efficient and yet graceful, and her throat went dry as she noticed the way his muscles moved beneath his shirt. He filled up the room with his presence, and at that moment she realized that she had fallen in love with him. He was everything she'd ever wanted in a man, and what's more, he was letting her set the pace, waiting for her to come to him.

He turned as though reading her thoughts and crossed the room. "Thank you for sharing your birthday with me." He kissed her softly, then pulled back to study her expression. "Ashley, I'd like to spend more time with you." He picked up her hand. "I'd like to know everything about you, your likes and dislikes, what makes you happy, what makes you sad." His eyes darkened. "I'd like to take our relationship to the next level, but not until you're ready. And I'm willing to wait." He pulled her toward him and she went willingly into his arms. "I love you, Ashley. I think I started loving you that first day on the ferry, crazy as that may sound."

"You're not crazy. Not crazy at all." She raised her lips and he kissed her with a tenderness that made her want to cry. Her whole world narrowed down to the man who held her, safe and secure in his strong arms and for a moment she thought she'd weep with happiness.

She didn't know whether to laugh or cry when the kettle whistled. "Kettle's boiling," she said, looking up at him with a mixture of longing and regret. "But you know something? I just realized how tired I am." She knew instinctively that he would understand her need to be alone, to think things through. "Would you mind taking me home?"

His eyes softened. "It *has* been a long day, and it's probably seemed even longer for that little dog of yours." He draped an arm round her shoulder. "Come on, sweet lady. I'll have you home in no time."

They made the short trip in companionable silence, and he walked her to the door and waited while she opened it. She watched his car pull away, hand at her throat as he waved from the top of the driveway. Turning slowly, she entered the house and picked up Honey, her thoughts churning. His words of love had opened a window to a world of new, exciting possibilities. She had been alone and emotionally shut off for long enough; it felt good to want to share her life again. Burying her face in Honey's coat she mounted the stairs to the loft. A kaleidoscope of images flashed through her mind as she drifted off to sleep. Every one of them was Matt.

The hummingbirds had become accustomed to Ashley's presence on the sundeck. They buzzed about as she sipped her coffee. She was due at a Little Theater meeting this morning, but for a few deliciously decadent moments she allowed herself to dream of a future with Matt. She picked up the souvenir picture of the balloon ride and she could almost feel the heat radiating off the field where it had been waiting to waft them away. She studied the two laughing faces in the picture. If they had been strangers, she would have said they were happy and very much in love. A cloud passed over the sun and she stood up abruptly, trying to shake off the sudden chill that enveloped her.

Ashley arrived a few minutes early for the meeting, but Lars and Fran were ahead of her, already settled in the corner booth. They waved her over and she threaded her way through the tables, smiling at the friendly faces that greeted her.

Fran scooted around and patted the seat beside her. "We were just talking about the living room set for the second act," she said, pushing her glasses up with her forefinger. "And I was saying that I'd show you how to do wallpaper."

Ashley nodded as the waitress offered to fill the mug in front of her and Roger arrived soon after. The discussion ranged from set decoration to construction. The others had worked behind the scenes before, and were knowledgeable about techniques and materials. With a clearer idea of her duties, Ashley relaxed and enjoyed the spirited conversation.

Agenda completed, the chatter soon veered away from the theater and back to the topic of offshore drilling. Ashley was appalled at the statistics relating to habitat loss and ecological damage, should an oil spill occur anywhere along the coast.

"What bothers me the most," said Roger, "is how they try to pass off our concerns by calling us alarmists and tree huggers. That really turns my crank." His eyes reflected his outrage as he looked around the table. "I've written letters, and urged everyone I know to do the same, but sometimes you just feel so damned helpless, if you know what I mean."

Ashley spoke quietly. "My friend Jessica Burns is an investigative journalist, and I called her the other night to see what, if anything, she can dig up. I should be hearing from her today or tomorrow." She looked at the others hopefully. "Maybe it's a false alarm."

"Let's hope so," said Lars, sliding out of the booth. "We'll be ready for you in a couple of days, Ashley. You can get started on the living room set." He reached into his pocket and tossed a generous handful of change on the table to cover his coffee. "I'd better get back to work before the boss sends out a search party." He smiled broadly. Lars and his wife were successful weavers and their work was much in demand. He wandered off, and Ashley smiled at his retreating back.

"I'd better get going as well," she said as she parted from Fran and Roger. "See you guys in a few days."

Ashley set a blank canvas on the easel and leafed through her numerous sketches. There were times when she knew precisely what she wanted to paint next; usually she couldn't wait to get started. But today she was listless and undecided. Staring at the blank canvas, she jumped when the telephone rang next to her.

"Statue?" Jessica's girlhood greeting made Ashley smile. "You sound far away."

"Just mentally," replied Ashley, "although I was off the island yesterday."

"So that's why I couldn't get you. I called and called to wish you happy birthday and did you answer? Nooo." She paused. "Trevor told me to stop getting my garters in a twist, that you were probably out with Matt. I almost brained him."

"You should have listened to him." A sigh slipped out and she could imagine her friend rolling her eyes. "We had the most perfect day, Jess."

"You mean better than the day we rode the big roller

coaster at the PNE and you threw up on my new shoes? This has gotta be good."

Jessica listened attentively as Ashley related the previous day's events. Eager to share the day with her friend, she spared no detail, the words spilling out like bright coins. When she finally caught her breath she realized that Jessica had been uncharacteristically quiet.

"You're quiet, Jess." The silence on the other end was becoming disconcerting. "This isn't like you. Don't you have some pithy remark about falling in love?" Ashley laughed nervously, waiting for her friend's inevitable comeback.

"Not right now, kiddo." Jessica's unexpected remark caught Ashley off guard and she sat down abruptly, her heart racing. "I dug into that offshore oil company you called about and it's not good news."

Ashley squeezed her eyes closed. Visions of orcas, dorsal fins slicing through the water, were replaced with those of oil spills and the deadly threat they posed. "I'm afraid to ask, Jess. What did you find out?" She tensed, waiting for the news.

"The company you mentioned, La Perouse Explorations, has been doing some serious lobbying to have the moratorium lifted, and it looks like they're getting very close to succeeding. Trouble is, every time there's a serious objection, the estimates of how much oil and gas are down there are raised." Ashley heard her fumbling with some papers. "I can't find the report right now, but the latest estimate was something like ten billion barrels of oil and forty trillion cubic meters of gas."

"That's a lot?" It might be a silly question, but Ashley had to ask.

"Oh yeah. And my sources tell me that even as we speak La Perouse is forging ahead as if lifting the moratorium is a done deal."

"La Perouse." The name sounded familiar. "Where have I heard that term before?"

"That's another thing." Jessica's scorn blazed through the phone. "They have the nerve to name their company after the fishing banks off the coast. La Perouse is the continental shelf that extends some forty miles off the coast of British Columbia. You could call it the Grand Banks of the Pacific Northwest." She paused, waiting for the information to sink in.

"But the fishing industry . . ." The enormity of what Jessica was saying was starting to sink in. "Orcas eat salmon. As a matter of fact, offshore orcas eat fish exclusively." She ran her fingers through her hair, as if to clear her mind. "Maybe one person can't make much difference, but I'm going to write to everybody I can think of about this. Can either you or Trevor do something? . . . You know, you could write an article, or maybe Trevor could do a television piece." Her thoughts swirled, anger and frustration threatening to overcome her normally calm approach to difficult situations.

"We've thought of that, and of course we'll run it up the flagpole, but La Perouse is in partnership with the two oil companies who own almost ninety percent of the drilling rights in the area, and between them, these corporations wield a lot of influence. We might do the best work of our lives but nobody is likely to print it, or in Trevor's case to air it, because they can't afford to lose their advertisers. It's a jungle out there, Ash."

"Yeah, and it's full of snakes."

"Speaking of snakes, there's something else." Jessica took a deep breath. "I did a company search on La Perouse and I found something you're not going to like. Matthew Ryan is on the board of directors."

Chapter Eleven

Ashley's world stopped turning as she tried to process what Jessica had just said. It couldn't be true. Not Matt. The man who'd taken her sailing couldn't possibly be connected with the company that now threatened the pristine waters around Vancouver Island. She opened her mouth to speak, but no words came out. She had never been physically struck in her life, but right now she felt as though she'd been punched in the gut.

"Speak to me, Ash."

"How could he?" The words came out as a raspy whisper and she scarcely recognized her own voice. "We went sailing up there and he didn't say a word. Not one word, Jess." She looked through the window, seeking a familiar object, a touchstone to ease the searing pain of betrayal. But there was nothing to grasp on to. Nothing made sense anymore.

"You know, I almost said something to Matt yesterday

on the way to Vancouver, but I wanted to wait until I had all the facts." The shock was starting to wear off and now anger was giving her strength. "I'm such a fool. I thought I could trust him. Who was I kidding? I mean, he's a tough businessman, right? What did that article say? The one you read to me? Something about him being a take-no-prisoners kind of guy?"

"Now come on, kiddo. He's been on the up-and-up so far."

She was too angry to listen. "Maybe that's what I wanted to think. Maybe I wanted to be swept off my feet. Why didn't I listen to that little voice in my head that was telling me to slow down?" She knew she was getting worked up, but she didn't care. "I should know better than to put my trust in someone too quickly." Pain sliced into her confidence, bringing her tirade to a sudden halt. "Oh, Jess, and I so wanted to believe in him!"

"Do you want me to come over and stay with you for a few days? I could get the first ferry in the morning."

Ashley shook her head even though her friend couldn't see her. "Thanks, but no. I need to be by myself for a while. Besides, we're starting on the sets for the theater pretty soon, so I'll be busy with that." A dull ache started to throb behind her eyes and she wandered into the kitchen for a glass of water and an aspirin. "I'll call you if I need to talk some more, okay?"

"All right, but please let me know if you want me to come over. Promise?"

"I promise, but I'll be okay. I really will. I just need some time to let this sink in and get my mind around it."

Ashley hung up and gravitated toward the deck, Honey

dancing excitedly around her feet. The enormity of what Jessica had told her started to sink in and she staggered to the top step, barely conscious of the little dog at her side. The warm body snuggled closer and a soft pink tongue licked her face. Ashley raised a hand to her face, unaware that she had been crying. Ignoring the tears, she gathered the dog onto her lap. "Sorry, but I just don't feel up to a walk on the beach today." Her gaze drifted along the shore to the tidal pools where she'd sketched Caitlin and Honey.

"I'm sorry, Caitlin," she whispered. "You did your best, but this Humpty Dumpty heart is more broken than ever."

She sat there while the shadows lengthened, staring into the distance. Fishing boats headed home with the day's catch and ferries chugged busily between the islands, but she looked through them into the recent past.

Painful as it was, she relived every moment of her time with Matt. From the first tentative conversation on the ferry right up until last night, and his declaration of love. How could she have so badly misjudged him? Why hadn't she listened to those niggling little doubts that had sneaked past the glow of contentment she'd pulled around herself like a warm blanket?

Why indeed? The answer was simple: because she hadn't wanted to hear them. She'd wanted happiness so much she'd ignored all the signs, convinced herself that dreams could come true.

She had only herself to blame. She'd let Matt sweep her off her feet, lapping up every word as he proclaimed his concern for the environment. But he was a businessman, a clever entrepreneur who was accustomed to getting his own way.

The more she thought about it, the angrier she became. Taking several deep breaths, she reached a decision. There was only one way to deal with this kind of treachery, and within moments she was on her way to his house, muttering under her breath as she rehearsed what she'd say to him.

She jabbed at the doorbell, irritated when there was no immediate response. She was about to turn away when he opened the door, his initial look of surprise giving way to one of pleasure.

"Ashley." His voice still had the ability to thrill her and she steeled herself for a confrontation. "I was just going to call you."

"And just what did you think you were going to say?" She had no idea this was going to be so difficult. Especially when he looked so appealing in a pair of shorts and T-shirt. She tried not to look at his muscled legs, ending in bare feet.

A perplexed frown furrowed his brow and he stepped back. "I was going to tell you how much I enjoyed yesterday, and ask you out for dinner tomorrow. Caitlin will be home anytime now, and I thought the three of us—"

"I don't think so." She waved him off as he opened the door wider, inviting her inside. "What I have to say won't take long." She was shaking with anger, and she bit down on her lower lip, hating the fact that tears were pooling in her eyes. "I trusted you, Matthew Ryan, I really did. How could you do this?"

"How could I do what?" He bent his knees, trying to see into her eyes. He reached toward her and she warded him off with raised hands.

"You took me up there sailing. You, you . . . you told me about the orcas, about their rubbing beach, about how they eat salmon." She dabbed at her eyes, determined not to break down before she'd finished what she came to say. "And yet the whole time you've been one of the directors of the company that's trying to get off-shore drilling rights."

He shook his head. "That's not true, Ashley."

"It isn't?" She wanted to believe him. She wanted to believe him so badly.

"No. La Perouse Explorations doesn't have the drilling rights. The oil companies have the drilling rights. La Perouse provides—"

"That's only semantics!" She glared at him. "However you slice it, you're still at the center of it." She turned her back, fighting for composure. "What hurts the most is that you didn't mention it once. Did you think I wouldn't find out, or did you think I wouldn't care?" She faced him again, her expression bleak. "We saw orcas. Magnificent creatures that were here long before we started destroying the planet with our dependence on oil, and yet you can let this happen."

Matt's first thought was that this was happening to someone else. Maybe this was what an out-of-body experience was like, he thought as he watched himself standing in the doorway, unable to speak. Ashley's distress was genuine, and yet he was unable to console her. His mind darted about, grasping and then discarding words of explanation, words of comfort. It was tearing him apart to see her like this—distraught, tears streaming down her face.

"I can't explain things right now, Ashley. I'm sorry."

"You can't explain." She threw up her hands. "Well that's a lot of comfort." She turned away and he had to stop himself from reaching out to her. He wanted to gather her up in his arms, to protect her from life's disappointments and to reassure her of his love. But he couldn't.

"So it's true, then?" she asked without turning around.

He searched his mind for something to tell her, but there was nothing. Nothing except the truth. "What is true is that La Perouse Explorations has been lobbying the government vigorously to lift the moratorium on offshore oil and gas exploration." It sounded like something out of an annual report, but it was the truth.

"And you're on the board of directors."

"Yes, I am. I'm coming to the end of my first five-year term this year." He looked beyond her to where the camp bus was coming up the drive.

"Well, that's just great." Her voice was dull, dispirited.

"Please, Ashley. I can't get into this right now."

The bus pulled up and Caitlin jumped down, running to her father. "Daddy, I had such a good time." Seeing the tense look on his face she turned to Ashley as her father walked over to the bus to retrieve her bag.

She tugged at Ashley's sleeve. "What's the matter?" Her small fingers grasped Ashley's hand and she looked back at her father, who stood silently, bag in hand. "Daddy?"

Ashley smiled weakly at Caitlin. "I'm sorry, sweetie. I'm a little upset right now." She shot a scathing look at Matt then crouched down, holding the confused young girl gently by the shoulders. "I'll see you later, okay?" She ran to her van, fumbling in her purse for her sunglasses, which she put on.

Matt watched her drive away, and for the first time in his life he wished that he could betray a confidence.

Caitlin turned to her father, a bewildered expression on her face. "What's the matter, Daddy?"

He reached down and took her hand, walking slowly up the steps and into the house. "It's really complicated, pumpkin."

Pulling her hand from his, Caitlin stopped and gave him a mutinous look. "I'm not a baby, Daddy." Her eyes pleaded for understanding.

Matt swung her up and sat her on the kitchen counter. Bracing his arms on either side of her, he gazed into her eyes. She regarded him soberly, waiting for him to speak.

"You know how I sometimes tell you I have to go to board meetings?" Caitlin nodded. "Well, there are times when we have to make really hard decisions at those meetings. Decisions that can affect a lot of people. Ashley has heard something that she doesn't agree with and she's pretty mad at me right now."

"Did you make a good decision, Daddy? Like when you told me about not doing things to other people if you don't want them to do the same thing to you?"

Matt smiled; she never ceased to amaze him. "Yes, I did. I made the only one I could."

"Then why is she mad at you?" Caitlin tipped her head to one side, clearly not understanding.

"That's the part that's complicated. Because of what she heard, she thinks she can't trust me."

"But she can trust you, Daddy. I know she can. Why didn't you tell her that?" The serious green eyes held his.

"I will, Caity, I will." He forced himself to smile. "And now I want to hear all about camp."

Ashley stared at her reflection in the mirror. Unable to sleep for the past two nights, she'd thrashed about, craving the sleep that would not come. Climbing listlessly into the shower, she let the water beat down until it turned cold. She had no idea how she'd be able to function at this afternoon's set-decorating workshop.

Padding out to the kitchen, she turned on the coffee then raised her eyes and looked outside. A ferry was disappearing behind the island to her west, and she smiled vaguely. Life was continuing all around her, and it was time to get back in the game.

"Thanks for taking the time to show me all this, Fran." Ashley was trying to keep up with the other woman as she pointed out where they kept the supplies. "I'm sure you're plenty busy learning your lines. How's that going?"

Fran laughed self-consciously. "I'm as nervous as all get-out, but they tell me that's normal." She opened a cupboard. "The paints are kept in here and I brought some sponges."

"Sponges." Ashley picked one up. "I've heard of sponge painting, but I've never tried it."

"Then you're in for a treat." Fran took a sponge out of the package and started tearing off bits, holding it out each time and looking at it critically.

"What are you creating?" Ashley was intrigued.

"These will be the pattern on the wallpaper." She dabbed her mutilated sponge in some paint and pressed it against a roll of newsprint. "See? Instant flower."

Ashley looked at it dubiously.

Fran repeated the process a few more times then ripped off the newsprint and walked to the other side of the room.

Ashley grinned. "From here it *does* look like a cluster of flowers.

"Right. You'll also need one or two smaller flowers and a couple of leaves. The carpenters have finished building the walls, so you can get started applying the base coat. After you've applied the color, you simply snap some vertical lines as a guide, and apply your 'flowers' in a repetitive pattern." She gave Ashley a nudge and a wink. "The thing to remember is that the audience doesn't see it close-up. It's meant to be wallpaper, and that's what they'll see."

Ashley practiced with the sponges, then worked steadily painting the walls. Waiting for that to dry, she sketched out her ideas for the scene that would appear through the window. She hadn't been near her easel for the past couple of days, but this was different and the creativity flowed unabated. For a couple of hours she pushed her heartbreak to the back of her mind and when Lars called her for a coffee break she was actually humming.

"So, was your friend able to ferret out any information on the drilling?" he asked, passing her a mug.

"I'm afraid so. The rumors are all too true." She blinked rapidly and turned away, stirring cream into her coffee.

"I'll be glued to the television tomorrow—that's for sure."

Ashley's head came up. "What for?"

"Haven't you heard? That exploration company . . . what's it called . . . La Perouse? They're holding a press conference in Vancouver. Evidently they plan to make a big announcement." He gave a short, humorless laugh. "As if we don't already know what they're going to say."

Ashley tried to appear calm, although her heart was jumping out of her chest. "I'd like to hear what they have to say. Do you know what time?"

"Four o'clock in the afternoon. Smart, huh? Perfect timing for the six o'clock news." He ground out his cigarette in the ashtray. "Do you know who Matthew Ryan is?"

Ashley opened her mouth to respond but Lars was off again, pacing around the room as he talked. "He's a big-shot computer tycoon. He lives here on the island, you know. Has a big estate at South Point. He's one of the directors of La Perouse and he'll be at the news conference." He whirled in her direction. "He built this community center, you know. Paid for every cent of it himself and made sure it was built with local labor."

For a moment Ashley thought Lars was softening, but he slammed a fist into the door frame. "Doesn't give him the right to put our coastal waters at risk, though."

He strode off, muttering to himself, and Ashley grabbed the counter for support. Matt had built the community center? She looked at the well-equipped kitchen through fresh eyes. But Lars was right. One building—albeit a much-needed one—didn't make up for Matt's involvement with La Perouse. She wandered back to the workshop, but she knew she wouldn't be able to concentrate. After a few minutes of uninspired effort she washed out her brushes and sponges and excused herself for the day.

"Did you hear, Jess? There's going to be a news conference tomorrow." Ashley paced around her living room, telephone gripped tightly.

"No flies on you, kiddo. I just heard about it myself." Jessica paused. "Matt's going to be there, Ash."

"I heard that too. I don't know if I can stand to watch it. Just seeing him again . . ." She stopped pacing. "Someone's at the door. Just a sec." Opening the door she was unprepared for the sight of Caitlin. She was wearing her purple backpack, and her bicycle was leaning against the house.

"Caitlin is here, Jess. I'll talk to you tomorrow."

"Okay, kiddo. I'll call you if I hear anything else."

Ashley smiled warmly at the young girl. "Hello, Caitlin. How are you?"

"Can I come in?" The child exhibited none of her usual confidence.

"Yes, of course. I was just headed out to the deck. You can join me." Ashley filled two glasses with juice and settled onto a deck chair. Honey looked from one to the other, then retired to her basket in the studio.

Caitlin sat opposite, swinging her feet and looking down into her glass. After a few moments she raised her head. "Are you mad at my daddy?" The green eyes regarded her solemnly. "He says you're upset about a decision he had to make." She was uncharacteristically still.

Ashley leaned forward and looked directly into Caitlin's eyes. She regretted that the youngster had come home while she was still there, that she'd seen her so close to tears. She might be angry with Matt, but she couldn't bring herself to hurt Caitlin. "Your dad and I disagree about something, Caity. It's an adult thing."

The child sighed. "He says you don't trust him anymore."

The back of Ashley's neck started to tingle as she considered Caitlin's words. "Did he say that?" She hated to pump the child for information, but she longed to hear anything that would prove her wrong.

"He said it was a hard decision, but that he made the right one." Caitlin got up and went to stand beside Ashley, one foot balanced on top of the other. "I love you, Ashley. I don't want you to be sad."

Ashley's eyes filled with tears and her arms went around the young girl. "I love you too, Caitlin." She looked over the child's head. *And I love your father as well,* she said to herself, *in spite of everything.*

"Do you think you and my daddy will be friends

again?" Caitlin fingered her necklace, and Ashley smiled at the memories it evoked.

"I hope so, sweetie. I really hope so. But right now I think it would be better if we don't see each other for a little while." Ashley's thoughts turned to the next day's press conference, and she crossed her fingers behind Caitlin's back.

Matt stood on his deck in the early morning sunlight, coffee mug in hand. His legendary composure had been stretched to the limit these past few days. Every time he took a moment for himself, he recalled Ashley at his front door, struggling not to cry as she confronted him. The memory haunted him, making his stomach churn. He reviewed the day ahead. Most of his time would be devoted to La Perouse and the afternoon's press confer-ence. He'd begun to regret his decision to accept a posi-tion on their board almost immediately upon making it. He didn't like their methods, but as the months had gone by he'd come to realize that by continuing to serve as a director, he could keep an eye on what they were doing, perhaps even be a positive influence. Time would tell. And today was that time.

"Hi, Daddy." Caitlin padded onto the deck in her pa-jamas and bare feet. "Are you going to work today?"

"Yes, pumpkin. Mike will be here to pick me up in a few minutes." He sat down at the table, where he could look into her eyes. "What are you going to do today?"

"I don't know, Daddy. Kimberly has gone away for a few days with her mom. Maybe I'll go for a bike ride around the island."

Matt sensed that there was something bothering his normally ebullient daughter. "Is something the matter, Caity?"

Caitlin mumbled a few words, her head lowered.

"What was that? I couldn't hear you."

His heart contracted as tears filled her eyes. He opened his arms and she crawled up on his lap, where he rocked her back and forth. Closing his eyes, he lowered his head, rubbing his cheek against the top of her head. They sat quietly for a moment until she squirmed and looked up at him.

"Ashley's sad, Daddy. I went to see her yesterday."

Matt's heart jumped into his throat. "Why didn't you tell me last night?" He wiped the tears from her cheeks.

"I didn't want to make you sad too." She rubbed her nose with the back of her hand. "I miss her, Daddy."

"So do I, pumpkin. I miss her a lot."

"I told her I love her and I hope she can be friends with you again." She gazed hopefully at her father.

"And what did she say about that?" Matt held his breath.

"She said she loves me too, and she hopes you can be friends again."

Matt smiled and kissed his daughter on the forehead. "Can you keep a secret?"

She nodded, eyes shining hopefully.

"I think that by the end of today we'll be friends again. What do you have to say about that?"

Throwing her arms around his neck, Caitlin gave him several enthusiastic kisses on the cheek. "That would be so excellent."

"Hold on, now." Matt was relieved to see that his daughter had regained her usual sparkle. "We have to sort out this business, but I'm hoping that we'll get that resolved today." They both looked up as the helicopter approached. "I'm going to be on television this afternoon, and I hope that after Ashley sees that, she'll understand that I made the right decision."

"Really? I'll watch you. What time? What channel?"

"It's at four o'clock, and Betty has all the info." The helicopter settled on the pad. "There's my ride. I have to go to work now, but I should be home for dinner and afterward we'll both go to visit Ashley."

Caitlin's upturned face glowed with happiness as the helicopter lifted off. By tonight, he hoped to see the same glow on Ashley's face. The helicopter gained altitude and he looked toward Vancouver, thinking of the day to come.

Ashley woke with a start. She'd been dreaming of Matt. They'd been floating in a balloon over the ocean, watching orcas leap out of the water for their benefit. With a rueful shake of her head she shook off the dream and climbed out of bed. A tingling sense of anticipation had replaced the anger she'd felt earlier and she looked forward to seeing him on television that afternoon and hearing what he had to say.

Sitting at her easel, coffee mug in hand, she tried to get motivated to work but it was no use. The only image she could keep in her mind was of Matt's face. She wanted desperately to see him again, but was it too late? With a resigned sigh she placed the paintbrush back in its holder and slid off the stool. The press conference seemed like a long time away, but until then she needed to keep busy. She headed to the community center, where she applied the first color on the walls and painted the trim. The next time she looked at her watch it was time to leave.

By four o'clock, Ashley was sitting anxiously in front of the television, a cup of tea clutched in her hands. The newscaster began her lead-in standing in front of a large visual depicting offshore drilling platforms. Striding up to the podium was Franklin Delahunt, the CEO of La Perouse. A confident older man with gray hair at his temples, he seemed at ease in front of the cameras. Flanked by Matt on one side, and a dark, slender man on the other, he started speaking.

"Ladies and gentlemen of the press, we have called this news conference to answer the public's concerns regarding the development of British Columbia's offshore oil and gas fields. As you know, the estimates of oil and gas are enormous, and it is our intention to unlock these valuable energy sources.

"Do we undertake this exploration with a profit motive? Absolutely. Let there be no mistake about that. Our shareholders expect us to protect and expand their investment, and we will do just that." He looked directly into the camera lens. "We also intend to supply our Pacific Rim customers with a steady supply of top-quality product at prices based on supply and demand, rather than on artificial cutbacks in production, which we all know are solely designed to drive up prices." He paused as cameras flashed and reporters scribbled in their notebooks. "At this time I would like to introduce the two gentlemen who share the podium with me this afternoon. To my right is Andrew Malone, CFO of La Perouse Explorations. To my left is Matthew Ryan, who has been the driving force behind some dramatic decisions regarding our drilling program."

Ashley leaned closer to the screen as Matt cocked his head to the side and looked up at the speaker, a wry smile on his face.

"I have asked these two gentlemen to be with me here today because they represent the conscience of oil and gas exploration in our province." He looked from one man to the other, a smile flickering briefly across his face. "As you know, there has been a public outcry regarding the dangers inherent in drilling in such an ecologically sensitive area as the La Perouse Banks. We are aware of these problems, and can assure you that, with today's technology and improvements in safety and equipment, we do not anticipate any, I repeat, *any,* environmental damage as a result of our drilling activities."

A murmur rippled through the crowd and he held up his hand. "I know you're thinking talk is cheap, and indeed it is, but at La Perouse we've decided to put our money where our mouth is." Turning to Matt, he smiled. "In recent weeks, Matthew Ryan has brought all of his considerable powers of persuasion to bear, single-handedly making a group of hardened businessmen see a new way of doing business." With a nod, he extended his hand and Matt rose, taking Frank's place.

Chapter Twelve

Gripping the podium with both hands, Matt looked at the assembled press corps, making eye contact with as many individuals as possible.

"Thank you, Frank. Ladies and gentlemen, Franklin Delahunt has granted me the pleasure of making this announcement today. He has proven to be a most enlightened CEO, and in my opinion, La Perouse will continue to flourish under his leadership."

Ashley caught a glimpse of the boyish grin she had grown to love. Matt took a deep breath and continued speaking.

"Many of you know that La Perouse has been lobbying for the lifting of the moratorium on offshore oil and gas exploration. One of the most sensitive areas in question is the continental shelf extending from the coast of British Columbia some forty miles out into the Pacific. This area is home to salmon of every species, as well as offshore orcas, who feed exclusively on fish."

He paused for a moment and Ashley found herself holding her breath.

"After many agonizing weeks of argument and discussion, the board of directors of La Perouse Explorations has decided *not* to pursue our present course of lobbying for the removal of the moratorium in the area for which our company is named."

The pressroom erupted in spontaneous applause and Ashley sat back in her chair, stunned. Matt stood at the podium, waiting for the sound to subside, then continued.

"We will also withdraw our request that oil tankers be permitted to sail closer to the mainland. As a matter of fact, we will join with the government in developing more programs to educate our youth about the importance of being environmentally conscious." He held up a hand.

"Now let me speak to all La Perouse shareholders, who are probably reeling with the implications of what I have just said. After all, the area for which our company is named represents some twenty percent of our rights, and that translates to an enormous sum of money. But let's be blunt here: If we were to exercise our rights in this particular location, the public backlash against our company would be immense. However, by voluntarily relinquishing our rights at La Perouse, we prove our concern for the environment in the most tangible way we know, and frankly, we feel that this will give us an advantage when the next set of talks is scheduled. In the long run, this decision is right for the company as well as for you, the shareholders, who can assure your children that you own shares in a company that did the honorable thing." He stood back from the podium and plunged his hands into his pockets, visibly relaxing. "It's been a difficult decision for all of us, and for me in particular, but I have always been confident that it would work out to the benefit of all concerned." He looked directly into the camera, and Ashley knew that he was speaking to her. She grabbed the phone and speed-dialed Jessica, keeping an eye on the press conference, where reporters were shouting questions at Matt. As she waited for her friend to answer, she heard his voice.

"The government has assured us that they will not transfer the rights to any other oil exploration company." He smiled into the camera, eyes crinkling. "After all, if La Perouse is going to give up this much profit, we don't want the competition to have a crack at it later."

Jessica picked up the phone, her voice jubilant. "What a fantastic turn of events!"

Ashley paced the floor, unable to contain her excitement. "I'm so proud I can't stand still. I just hope I didn't ruin everything when I went over there and blasted him."

"Come on, kiddo, give him a little credit."

"I don't know, Jess. I was pretty steamed."

"Did he tell you to go away and never come back?"

Ashley winced. "No, I didn't give him a chance. I just stormed off." She frowned to herself. "Why didn't he just tell me?"

"Could be a couple of different reasons. Perhaps they were still undecided. But I suspect the main reason was that it's a publicly traded company. No matter what kind of a spin they put on it, this decision is going to affect their share price, at least in the short term. It probably killed him not to be able to say anything, but he couldn't."

Ashley absorbed her friend's words. "No, of course not. I can see that now."

"So what's next between you guys? Are you going to rush over there and beg his forgiveness? Groveling always works for me at a time like this."

Ashley laughed, feeling light and carefree for the first time in days. "I'll think of something, but in the meantime I'm just relieved."

"All I can say is that's one heck of a guy you've got there. I think you should go for it. Tell him how you feel." Jessica's voice was warm and supportive. "Call me soon, okay?"

"I will, Jess. And thanks."

Ashley couldn't stop smiling. She pumped a fist in the air and took a few exuberant dance steps around the deck. The telephone buzzed and she picked it up.

"I'm sorry to bother you, Mrs. Stewart, but have you seen Caitlin today?"

Ashley's impromptu dance halted when she heard the concern in the housekeeper's voice.

"She was here yesterday, but I haven't seen her today. I was out for a couple of hours earlier, but there's no sign of her having been around. Is something wrong?"

"She was going to be home by four o'clock to watch her father on television. It's already past five and there's no sign of her. I'm getting worried, and Archie's in town so I should stay here in case she comes home."

"Did she tell you where she was going?" Ashley's mind was racing.

"No, she didn't. All she said was that she was going for a ride, but that was right after lunch. I can't imagine what's keeping her."

It was hard not to imagine the worst, but Ashley reined herself in. "I'll be right over. Maybe I can start looking for her." Ashley disconnected and gathered up Honey, who squirmed happily in anticipation of going for a ride in the car.

Ashley searched her mind for places that Caitlin might be. The island was small, but there were plenty of side roads where a child might venture. As she pulled into Matt's driveway, her cell phone rang.

"Ashley, it's Matt. Caitlin is missing. Have you seen her?"

"No, I haven't. Betty called me and I'm just arriving at your place now." She pulled up by the front door and turned off the motor. "I'll start looking right away." All thoughts of the press conference had vanished.

"This isn't like her, Ashley. I'm worried. I'm in the helicopter now and we've just left my building. The pilot says we'll be there in about eighteen minutes."

She could imagine only too well the terror that Matt must be experiencing and she tried to sound confident. "We'll find her, Matt. I'll touch base with Betty first and see you later."

The housekeeper was walking down the steps as Ashley jumped down from the van. "Thank you for coming, Mrs. Stewart. Matthew is on his way back now but I'm so worried." There was a smudge of flour on her cheek and her hands were bunched up in her apron. "If anything has happened to her . . ."

Ashley guided the distraught woman into the kitchen. "Tell me again. Did she say anything . . . anything at all about where she was going?"

"No, just that she was going for a bike ride." She looked about distractedly, and her gaze landed on Ashley's painting, propped up on the mantel.

Ashley followed the other woman's line of sight. Caitlin's fascination with marine life might have led her to find more tidal pools. Digging through her memory, she tried to recall what Caitlin had told her on one of her visits. Hadn't she said something about a special place?

"That's it!" she said aloud, heading toward the door. She paused and looked back at the housekeeper. "When Matt gets here, tell him I've gone to look for Caity around East Side road. I think she and her little friend found some tidal pools over there."

Hope bloomed on the housekeeper's face. "Right, then. Off you go."

Ashley was soon back on the main road that circled the island. Where was that spot she'd noticed before? "It's along here somewhere," she murmured aloud, slowing down and watching for glimpses of water through the trees. The shoreline looked different this afternoon and she realized that the tide was in, changing the shape of some of the bays. An opening loomed just ahead and she slowed even more, creeping along, looking for a familiar landmark. The low afternoon sun bounced off the water into her eyes, but the long spit of elevated land was still there. The area looked different today, and it took her a moment to realize that the connecting causeway had been covered by the incoming tide.

Coming to a halt, she recognized Caitlin's bike slumped against a tree. If she hadn't known to look, she'd never have spotted it. Setting the brake, she jumped out, her mind focused on finding Caitlin. Honey was out the door and beyond her grasp before she could react. The dog ran to Caitlin's bicycle, sniffed at it, then bounded toward the shore.

Pushing aside the thick undergrowth and crawling over deadfalls, Ashley made her way to the water's edge. The tide surged through the narrow passageway, swirling alarmingly as it reached its peak.

"Caitlin," she called, then louder. "Caitlin!"

The sound of water lapping against the rocks muffled her calls. "Caitlin!" she repeated, then stopped to listen for a response. Thinking she heard a faint response, she called again. Honey hadn't moved from her spot at the edge of the water. She stood at point, legs stiff and head alert. Then without warning, she plunged into the water and started to swim the narrow channel between the shore and the elevated finger of land. Ashley watched in horror as the small dog struggled against the tide, but she was a strong swimmer and a few minutes later she was standing on the shore, shaking water from her coat. Picking her way around the driftwood, which lay haphazardly on the rocks, she disappeared into the scrub.

"Well, that's just great," she said aloud. "First Caitlin and now Honey." She was about to call again when

Matt pulled up on the road and crashed down to the shore through the undergrowth.

He touched her briefly and she looked up at him. He appeared to have aged in the few hours since she'd seen him on her television screen. "Honey just took off." She pointed to the low, scrub-covered point of land. "She swam across there and disappeared into those bushes."

"Caitlin!" Matt's voice was loud, his call urgent.

Honey bounded out through the bushes, her tail wagging. Caitlin was next, her purple backpack a vivid slash of color among the vegetation. "Daddy!" she called across the water, limping forward with the aid of a stick. "I knew you'd come."

Matt strode into the water and Ashley held her breath as the current swirled around him, but the water only rose to his chest, and he was across in less than a minute. He picked up his daughter and held on to her tightly, kissing her face over and over. "Oh, Caity," he cried, "I was so worried about you."

"I'm sorry, Daddy. I didn't watch the tide and then I slipped and hurt my foot." She looked at him proudly. "But I had my water bottle in my backpack and I knew that the tide would go down pretty soon." She looked down at the dog. "Honey found me, Daddy." She looked across the water and waved at Ashley.

Matt waded across the channel carrying his precious cargo. He turned to look back for Honey, but she was already swimming strongly behind them, reaching the shore moments later. She gave a mighty shake then stood on her hind feet, pawing at Matt's leg to get closer to Caitlin. Matt reached down and petted her, his face wreathed in smiles.

"Let's get you both home and out of those soaking clothes." Ashley led the way back to the road.

Matt deposited Caitlin in the Land Rover, then came back to Ashley. Looking deeply into her eyes, he brushed a hand against her cheek. "See you back at my place?" She nodded. "Good, 'cause we have things to talk about."

Betty and Archie hovered in the driveway as the two vehicles came to a stop by the front door. "There you are, my angel." Betty held Caitlin's face in both hands. "Are you all right?"

Caitlin seemed taken aback by all the fuss. "Yes, thank you. I twisted my ankle, but it's feeling better already." She grinned sheepishly. "Honey and Daddy rescued me. I'm sorry if I upset you."

"Gracious me. Don't you be sorry about that." The housekeeper looked at Matt's soaking clothes. "Perhaps you should have a shower to warm up. I'll run a bath for Caitlin and have a look at her foot."

Matt disappeared in the direction of his bedroom, and Ashley wandered out onto the deck. Suddenly exhausted, she sat down in a chair and Honey flopped down at her feet, resting her head on her two front paws. Leaning back, she closed her eyes, searching for the right words to offer Matt as an apology.

"I was hoping to have a few minutes alone with you." Matt appeared at her side, freshly showered and clothed in navy sweats and a loose T-shirt. His hair was still damp, and it shone like ripe wheat in the golden light from the setting sun.

Ashley stood up, needing to face him. There were no magic words, no silver bullet to make this right. Only the plain, unvarnished truth would do. "Matt, I'm sorry about the other day. I . . ."

He shook his head slowly. "No, my sweet. You have nothing to be sorry about." He gazed into her eyes, and her knees weakened with the love she saw on his face. Cupping her cheek with a hand, he ran a thumb across her lips, sending a shudder of desire coursing through her body. "Did you see the press conference today?"

Ashley nodded.

"I'm so glad that's behind me." He pulled her into his arms. "Not being able to tell you about what I was proposing was really hard. When you left here that day thinking I'd betrayed you it almost broke my heart. But I couldn't tell you, Ashley. I simply couldn't betray a confidence."

"I understand, Matt. Really I do. I should have known you'd do the right thing and I feel guilty for doubting you." She pulled back and looked up at him. "I've been so worried that I'd lost you."

"Never." He lowered his head and brushed her lips with his. "You could never lose me, Ashley. Don't you know that?" His mouth covered hers, and she lost herself in the pleasure of his kiss. His lips were gentle and demanding at the same time, claiming her mouth. Her arms went around his neck.

"Excuse me, Matthew." Betty stood in the doorway, a broad smile on her face. "Caitlin is finished with her bath and she's asking for you both."

Matt draped his arm around Ashley's shoulder and

they went upstairs to Caitlin's bedroom, followed by Honey.

The child's eyes lip up as she saw them in the doorway. Then her eyes were drawn to the dog at their feet. "Can Honey come up on the bed, Daddy? She's almost dry."

Matt and Ashley smiled at each other. "All right, pumpkin. Just this once."

Caitlin patted the side of the bed and the dog jumped up, wriggling along the duvet until her body was stretched out beside her new friend. "Betty says I should be able to walk around tomorrow, but that I should stay close to home for a few days."

"Sounds like a good plan." Matt sat down on the side of the bed and smoothed the child's hair away from her face. "I'm taking a few days off, myself. We have a few things to straighten out around here."

Caitlin's sleepy eyes looked from her father to Ashley. "Are you friends again?"

Ashley leaned over and gave her a hug. "Yes we are. Everything's going to be just fine."

"Good," she said, snuggling down in her bed. "We love you, Ashley."

A lump formed in Ashley's throat. "I love you too, Caity."

Matt leaned over his daughter and kissed her good night. She draped her arm around the dog and was fast asleep before they left the room.

Matt guided Ashley into the kitchen. "Do you mind?" he said, indicating a computer in a small alcove. "I want to make sure my secretary managed to cancel my appointments for the next few days."

"Not at all." Ashley picked up the kettle. "Tea?"

Matt nodded, distracted by his messages. "Well, what do you know?" he said after a moment.

"What is it?" Ashley was setting a couple of mugs on a tray.

"Several stock analysts have come out already recommending a buy on La Perouse stock. It'll be interesting to see what happens when it opens tomorrow."

"Well, what do you expect? With you on the board, how could they lose?"

"I'm not even sure I want to remain on the board. Would you like a fire?"

Ashley laughed. "You're beginning to sound like your daughter. Jumping from one subject to another at warp speed. But yes, I'd like a fire."

They settled into the luxuriously soft leather of a large sofa, the tea tray on an ottoman in front of them.

"Do you have to decide immediately?" asked Ashley. "About remaining on the board?"

"That's a tough one. I didn't care for their lobbying tactics, but if I stay I can keep an eye on them."

"Never mind. You'll do what's right." Ashley poured tea and handed him a mug.

"It would be a lot easier if I didn't have to make that decision alone."

She gave him a long, questioning look. "What do you mean?"

Everything was moving slowly, as in a dream. A log crackled in the fireplace, sending a shower of sparks up the chimney, but neither of them noticed. Music played in the background, a romantic sound track for the beginning of their life together.

"I love you," he said, "and I'm willing to wait as long as it takes, but someday I'd like us to be together. You, Caitlin, and me. And Honey, of course."

"We'd be a family," she said, her heart in her throat. She moved into his arms and their lips met with all the longing and desire that had built up over the past few agonizing days.

When they finally pulled apart, he searched her face for an answer. "Well, what do you think?" he asked, his voice raspy with emotion.

"A family," she repeated softly, touching his face with her fingertips. "With a man and a little girl I already love." A sigh of contentment escaped her lips. "It's all I've ever wanted."